GREVY DANGER

A KENYA KANGA MYSTERY

VICTORIA TAIT

Dedication
I'd love to thank the first readers who contacted me to tell me how much they enjoyed my story.

Those initial emails meant so much, and still do!

To Pat Brewerton, Linda Gonzales,
and the two Jeans,
Jean Curtis, in South Africa, and Dr Jean Lowery.

For more information visit VictoriaTait.com

PHRASEOLOGY

STYLE, SPELLING AND PHRASEOLOGY

Mama Rose, the main character through whose eyes we view events, has a British education and background. She uses British phrases, spelling and style of words.

Kiswahili words are also used in the book and most are linked to a Glossary at the back, which briefly explains their meaning.

These words add to the richness and authenticity of the setting and characters, and I hope increase your enjoyment of Grevy Danger.

STYLE & KISWAHILI GLOSSARY

The main character, Mama Rose, has a British upbringing and she uses British phrases.

Kiswahili words are used to add to the richness and authenticity of the setting and characters, and most are linked to this Glossary.

- *Amref* Kenyan medics and flying doctor service
- *Asante* Thank you
- *Askari* Watchman/Security Guard
- *Ayah* Kenyan nanny
- *Bahati* Luck(y)
- *Bahati Njema* Good Luck

- *BATUK* British Army Training Unit Kenya
- *Boda Boda* Motorbike used as a taxi
- *Bwana* Sir, a term of respect used for an older man
- Chai Tea made by boiling leaves / tea bag with milk (and sugar).
- Chamgei Hello in Kalenjin
- *Daktari*. Doctor
- *Habari* Greeting used like hello but meaning 'What news?'
- *Habari Yako?* How are you?
- *Hapana* No
- *Kanga* Colourful cotton fabric (also Swahili for guinea fowl)
- *Kikoi* Brightly coloured cotton garment or sarong
- *Kikuyu* Kenyan ethnic group or tribe
- *Kongoi* 'Thank you' in Kipsigis dialect
- *KSPCA* Kenya Society for the Protection & Care of Animals
- *KWS* Kenya Wildlife Service
- *Maisha Marefu* Cheers
- *Memsaab/Memsahib* Madam / White woman, often an a position of authority
- *M-Pesa* Mobile money - transferred between phones

- *Muram* Gravel road
- *Mzuri* Good
- *Mzuri Sana* Very Good
- *Mzungu* European / White person
- *Pole* Sorry (Pronounced Pow-lay)
- *Punda Milia* Zebra
- *Sawa (sawa)* Fine, all good, no worries.
- *Shamba* Vegetable patch / garden (or farm)
- *Shuka* Thin, brightly coloured blanket in bright checked colours, where red is often the dominant colour. Also used as a sarong or throw
- *Stoney Tangawizi Ginger Beer* - a popular brand of ginger beer.
- *Tafadhali* Please
- *Tusker* Popular Brand of Beer

OTHER TERMS

- *Car Park* Parking Lot

CAST OF CHARACTERS

"Mama Rose" Hardie
Community vet & silver-haired amateur sleuth
Thabiti Onyango
Anxious young African man & friend of Rose's childhood friend, Aisha, now deceased
Pearl Onyango
Thabiti's sister who suffered mentally after her mother's death
Chloe Collins
30-something British woman, who recently moved to Kenya
Dr Emma
Vet, who is technically Rose's boss
Marina
Young Indian woman & Thabiti's love interest

Authorities

Commissioner Akida Nanyuki Police Commissioner

Constable Wachira (Judy) Young, intelligent police officer

Sam Mwamba Officer in the Kenya Wildlife Service, member of Kenya's Anti-Corruption Unit & Constable Wachira's love interest

Ms Fatima Rotich Nanyuki's newly appointed Coroner

Dr Farrukh Female half of the Drs Farrukh, who work at The Cottage Hospital

Sergeant Muthoni From Isiolo Police station

Newton Family

Hellen Newton Opened and runs Jengo Real Estate office in Nanyuki

Alex Newton Partner in Horizon Safaris, a family business

Mia Newton Young Daughter

Liam Newton Toddler aged son

Tessa Newton Alex's sister, who works as an independent safari guide

Munro & Ramsey Families

Rebecca Munro (Becky) mid-20s, born in Kenya but living on the UK

Eloise Ramsey Rebecca's sister, married to Guy

Guy Ramsey Partner, with Alex Newton, in Horizon Safaris

Fergus Peacock Family lawyer, based in Nairobi

Michael Munro (Mick) Rebecca & Eloise's father, who is missing

Geraldine Munro Rebecca & Eloise's mother, who is missing

Nanyuki Residents (& Others)

Kipto Rose's house girl

Chumba Kipto's grandson

Samwell Rose's stockman

Pete Stephenson Plane hunter

Mrs Winnie Sharpe Elderly lady who is robbed

Otto Wakeman Young polo player

Sophia Gilbert Young polo player

Reggie Usman Thabiti and Pearl's Father

Dan Collins Chloe's husband, who works away from home most of the time

Poppy Chambers East Africa Women's League, & wife of Dickie Chambers

Dora East Africa Women's League

Birdie Rawlinson East Africa Women's League

Craig Hardie Rose's recently deceased husband
Chris Hardie Rose's son, living in England
Heather Rose's daughter, living in England

CHAPTER ONE

R ose Hardie leaned against an uneven post-and-rail fence under the waning afternoon sun. She scratched her head of fuzzy white hair as she watched Bette, her jersey cow, grazing beside her old horse, Whoosh, and Bahati, a pony recently rescued from the side of a busy road in Nairobi, Kenya's capital.

Her gaze was drawn to the majestic peak of Mount Kenya, under whose shadow her home town of Nanyuki had been established a hundred years before.

She was known locally as 'Mama Rose' because of her work over the past forty years as a community vet. She'd stitched wounds, administered injections and treated the diseases of countless domestic and farm animals. She'd also tended to a range of Kenyan wildlife, from tortoises to elands.

Sixty-five year old Rose and had been born and raised in Kenya. She sighed, thinking of her husband, Craig, who had died recently after suffering a complication to the polio he had contracted as a child and a series of strokes. But she was thankful, knowing how lucky she had been to find mutual love and respect in her marriage.

When they first met, over forty years ago, Craig was a young accountant who'd recently arrived from Scotland. He'd been quiet and gentle but strong, and he'd helped her overcome her personal troubles.

Her father had been persuaded to sell the family farm during independence, so after their marriage she and Craig had moved around the highlands of Kenya as Craig earned a living as a farm manager. They both relished life out on Kenya's open expanses of savannah alongside Africa's wonderful array of wildlife.

"Are you thinking of Bwana Craig, Mama?" asked an African woman, with deep lines scored into her face, as she joined Rose beside the fence.

"Yes, he loved Kenya. Its beauty and its quirks." Rose smiled warmly at Kipto, her house girl.

Izzy, Rose's one-eyed black and white cat, jumped onto the fence beside them and slowly picked her way along the top rail. She sprang to the ground and stalked along a black netted enclosure where Rose grew medicinal plants and flowers.

She'd developed recipes for a range of herbal mixes which she sold to horse owners. The money supplemented her veterinary income. In an adjacent enclosure she grew vegetables to feed herself and her staff.

"Bwana die happy man, I think. It was his time." Kipto nodded her head, as if agreeing with her own statement.

Rose rolled her shoulders and replied, "I'm sure you're right. But I still miss him."

Her gaze moved away from her small paddock as she looked across at her thatched, one-bedroom cottage. Should she fix the leaking roof above the kitchen, or inform her landlord? She didn't want to make life difficult for him as the rent on her cottage, and accompanying garden and paddock, was very reasonable.

She couldn't afford a similar sized property in Nanyuki as rents were rising as the town expanded. This was due partly to more British army soldiers arriving to work at the growing military base, but Kenyan families were also leaving Nairobi seeking a quieter and healthier life in the small market town.

She considered the rickety wooden garage as she said to Kipto, "Can you remind me to speak to Thabiti about selling Craig's Subaru? There's no point keeping two cars, and I can use the money to repair the kitchen roof and service my Land Rover."

She thought of the three invoices lying on the desk in Craig's office. She would receive some money from the government towards Craig's hospital treatment, but she still had to find the funds for the outstanding balance, and for his cremation and wake. Should she ask Chris and Heather to contribute towards their father's bills?

Chris had left immediately after his father's memorial service, but Heather had stayed with her for a week before returning to the UK. They'd spent most of their time sharing memories which had helped Rose begin her grieving process.

Heather had always been Craig's favourite, even before he and Chris became estranged. Rose hadn't exactly been jealous of the father-daughter relationship, but there were times when she'd felt excluded.

She remembered, with fondness, the precious few days she'd spent together with Heather as they'd reconnected, and she now felt closer to her daughter and her family. Maybe she should visit them in the UK, but not in winter. The cold, damp, grey British winter days were too depressing and would only exaggerate her arthritis. Perhaps next Easter, or in May when her granddaughters had a week's break from school.

Rose watched Potto, her black and tan terrier, dash into the field.

Rose smiled. This was the simple life which she enjoyed so much. Looking around her, she accepted that she owned very little but a few possessions and her precious memories. She thought of the first epistle of Paul to Timothy in the Bible, "For we brought nothing into the world, and we can take nothing out of it."

Her contemplation was broken by the ringing of her mobile phone.

CHAPTER TWO

R ose pushed open the door of Dr Emma's pharmacy in the centre of Nanyuki. She carried a plastic bag which contained a flask of fresh thyme tea, a pot of natural yoghurt and a small bag of flour. Dr Emma had requested the strange assortment.

"Thank you for coming," said a petite, white-gowned African lady with bright yellow glasses and an enormous head of black hair, which she allowed to grow naturally into an Afro style. This was Dr Emma, and she was holding a cotton pad against a small mound of fur, which was laid on top of some towels on a white plastic table.

Dr Emma was officially Rose's boss. She ministered to small animals in her pharmacy and preferred to leave larger animals, and those who could not be brought into Nanyuki, to be treated by Rose. The pharmacy also served as an examination room and an operating theatre when required.

The white plastic table normally displayed dog bowls, cat baskets and a red hamster cage, but it was cleared when animal patients needed assessing and treating.

"Will it be all right?" asked Poppy Chambers, in a hoarse voice, as she looked down at a cream and brown hamster lying dejectedly on the table. The cotton pad Dr Emma held against it was stained red with blood.

Rose approached Poppy and put a hand on her friend's shoulder.

"You see, it's not ours," Poppy continued. "My granddaughter's class at Podo School had a 'bring your pet to school day'. But her hamster, Fuzzy, attacked this one when they were both let out of their cages."

"Let's take a look. I think the bleeding has slowed," Dr Emma said as she carefully removed the pad. When she touched the hamster to examine its wound, it squeaked and flinched. She looked up and said, "There's a loose flap of skin which will need stitching back into place."

"But how will you do that? It's so small." Poppy's voice wavered with uncertainty.

"First things first," replied Dr Emma. She looked at Rose and asked, "Did you bring the items I asked for?"

Rose handed over the plastic bag and replied, "I did, but I've no idea what they're for."

"After Mrs Chambers called me I looked up small rodent treatments and taking a page out of your book, considered the more 'natural' remedies." Dr Emma placed the items from the bag onto the counter behind her.

"Firstly, hamsters react badly to many antibiotics and they are also difficult to inject." She opened the pot of yoghurt and drew a small amount into a syringe.

"Mama Rose can you hold the hamster still?" Dr Emma asked as she gently pressed the syringe into the side of the animal's mouth and steadily pushed down the plunger. The hamster squirmed and the syringe fell out.

"I think I gave it enough," said Dr Emma as she deposited the syringe into a miniature flip-topped dustbin. "The yoghurt is a source of live, naturally occurring bacteria which will help fight any infection it has."

She reached for the flask and revealed, "Next I'm going to use the thyme tea as an antiseptic to clean the wound."

"Yoghurt? Thyme tea? But they're not proper medicines. How will they help?" Poppy ran a hand through her neatly cut dark hair, which contained streaks of grey.

Dr Emma poured some tea into a cup and explained, "Small rodent owners swear by them as they are far less invasive, and don't cause the side effects that standard medications often do."

She dipped a Q-Tip, normally used for cleaning out someone's ear canal, into the thyme tea and passed it to Rose. "Can you swab the wound?"

Rose held the small hamster and gently swabbed the damaged area while Dr Emma once more pushed a syringe into its mouth. "I'm giving it a small anaesthetic, Mrs Chambers, to dull the pain while I stitch it. Mama Rose, when you've finished, can you sprinkle a little of the flour over the wound."

"I wondered what that was for," admitted Rose. "You have been busy researching alternative medical treatments."

"It's very interesting. Flour encourages the blood to clot and should reduce bleeding as I suture the wound." Dr Emma pulled on a fresh pair of blue latex gloves. "I think a normal hook-shaped needle is too large. So I'll try this domestic one, but I'll have to hold it by hand."

Rose held the hamster steady as Dr Emma leaned over it. She held the flap of skin between her forceps and pushed the needle through. She repeated the action, reattaching the damaged flap of skin. Whilst Dr Emma worked methodically and carefully along the wound, the hamster remained calm and quiet.

"Do you really need my help?" Rose asked, "or is this hamster just an excuse to check up on me?"

Dr Emma didn't look up. "A bit of both, really. I wasn't sure how I would manage as I've never attempted to stitch such a small animal. But I did want to reassure myself that you're coping. Are you?"

"I think so. I haven't felt like going out and meeting people, so I've been steadily getting on with things at home. I've been working in my shamba, and Kipto and I have sorted through most of Craig's belongings."

Rose turned to Poppy and commented, "I did enjoy Dickie's eulogy. Sometimes it's difficult to look past Craig's illness and remember him when he was fit and active. Your husband included some marvellous stories, some of which I hadn't heard before."

Poppy responded with a gentle smile. "Craig was a dear friend of Dickie's. Has he told you about the portrait?"

Rose nodded. "One of Craig to be hung in the polo club? It's a wonderful idea, and Craig would have been so proud. And Dickie's suggested I present a trophy at next month's Mugs Mug Polo Tournament in Craig's memory."

"If you do feel like catching up with friends, we have a Women's League meeting this Thursday." Poppy turned to Dr Emma and asked, "Why don't you join us?"

Dr Emma concentrated on her stitching.

Rose laughed. "Despite her outgoing nature, I suspect our good doctor is intimidated by the League's members."

"I don't think anyone has ever described little Dora as intimidating, but I suppose there's a reason Dickie calls us the monstrous regiment of women."

Dr Emma looked up. "I'm nearly done." Her attention returned to her patient. "I also wanted to see you to discuss an idea I have."

"What idea?" Rose asked hesitantly.

"I heard a rumour that a Nairobi-based veterinary practice is looking for premises in Nanyuki."

"That's hardly surprising when you consider how much Nanyuki has grown in the past five years," remarked Poppy.

"Exactly," agreed Dr Emma, "and the new British army families, and those who've moved up from Nairobi, expect a professional service and not someone operating, literally, in a small shop."

"So what are your options?" Rose enquired.

"I spoke with the lady working at the new real estate office, next to Dormans coffee shop. And she said she'd see what suitable properties are available. But what do you think?"

Rose considered Dr Emma's question.

"You're right about the town expanding," Poppy agreed. "Have you heard about the proposed new shopping centre on the Laikipia road?"

"No," replied Rose, wondering what else she had missed whilst she'd been grieving for Craig.

Poppy's eyes sparkled as she explained, "An upmarket supermarket chain is supposed to be interested in taking space. And there will be restaurants, and possibly even a cinema."

"In that case, as even more people will be tempted to move to Nanyuki, I think you're right to look for new premises," confirmed Rose. "But won't that mean more work? How will you cope?"

Dr Emma cut the thread of the final stitch and stood up rolling her shoulders. "I think I can manage for the moment. But if I open a proper operating theatre I will need someone with operation and anaesthesias experience. And I know that many of the farmers and horse people have been asking you for a mobile X-ray unit."

"It's a lot to think about, and what about the cost?" Rose asked.

Dr Emma sighed. "I've a small amount of savings. For the moment I think I'll just look for new premises, but be aware of having room to expand in the future. If you're interested I'll let you know if and when I have a property to view."

Rose brightened. "Yes, please do. I love looking around other people's land and property."

CHAPTER THREE

The small hamster looked forlorn lying on the white plastic table in Dr Emma's pharmacy. Its paws twitched.

"It's waking up," observed Dr Emma, "but I think we should wait a bit before you take it back to its owner. Why don't you sit down?"

She collected two green plastic stools from the back of the shop and handed them to Rose and Poppy.

"You mentioned the lady working at the new real estate office. I think her children are at Podo School," said Poppy.

Dr Emma picked up a business card up from the pharmacy counter and read out loud, "Hellen Newton, Jengo Real Estate, Nanyuki Branch."

"That's right," agreed Poppy as she sat down. "Her husband Alex took over Horizon Safaris when his father died." She lowered her voice. "Apparently his sister wasn't at all happy as she thought the business should have been hers. She even hijacked some clients in Amboseli National Park after a row with her brother. So now she works as an independent tour guide."

"I thought that philanderer Guy Ramsey was involved with Horizon Safaris," said Dr Emma. She laid a small cloth over the hamster so only its head was visible.

Poppy leaned forward. "Guy Ramsey bought into the business a few years ago. And it's a poorly kept secret that he did so with his wife's money. But then he probably felt entitled to it since his wife's grandfather supposedly swindled his family out of their land and fortune."

"Who is his wife?" asked Rose.

"Her maiden name was Eloise Munro. You must remember her parents, Mick and Geraldine? They lived in Nyeri but disappeared a few years ago."

"I know who you mean," said Dr Emma. "Didn't their plane crash on the Aberdare Range?"

"That's the general view, although the wreckage has never been found."

Rose did remember. "Didn't they leave two daughters?"

Poppy nodded. "Eloise, who married Guy, is the older daughter. Her younger sister, Rebecca, was studying in England at the time and she stayed on after her parents vanished. But I'm sure I saw Eloise in Nanyuki yesterday, with a younger woman bearing a strong resemblance to her. I thought it might be Rebecca."

Dr Emma pulled a chair around from behind the counter and sat down. She mused, "Hellen Newton said her husband's business partner, and his wife and sister-in-law, were staying with them."

Poppy clasped her hands in front of her. "There we are then. It must have been Rebecca Munro. Do we know where Hellen Newton is living? I should pop round with a house-warming present."

CHAPTER FOUR

Thabiti rode his mountain bike down the rough earthen path. He was an African man, in his early twenties, who had become acquainted with Mama Rose and Craig after his mother had been killed. Rose had helped him investigate and identify his mother's murderer.

He ducked down against the handles of his bike. Although the eroded track was lower than the grass banks, he was still apprehensive about the single strand of thick elephant wire. It hung across the path, and acted as a deterrent against elephants leaving the forested area of Mount Kenya in search of food from the myriad of small fields beyond.

The path wound between tall maize stalks and their sea of long, slender leaves obscured his view as he rode around a bend. He grabbed at his brakes and skidded to a stop. A ragged goat ignored him as it stretched its neck and strained to reach a bowed head of unripe corn, but its tethering rope was pulled taught across his path.

He dismounted but hesitated before tugging at the rope. The goat abandoned its quest and with an air of indifference wandered back across the path.

Thabiti remounted. He wore a pair of baggy tan coloured cycling shorts, a matching short-sleeved t-shirt, and a black cycling helmet, with a visor to shield his eyes from the sun.

As he ducked under the elephant wire again, and re-entered the forest area, he spotted his sister, Pearl, and their friend, Chloe, jogging along a track towards a clearing on the edge of the mountain.

He admired his sister and wondered at her transformation from skinny socialite, who spent most of her time in beauty spas and at parties, to a limp and unresponsive shadow, after their mother's death, to this strong, athletic figure.

She slowed to walk as they all converged on the forest clearing.

Pearl bent over and stretched her hands to the ground as she gasped, "My trip to India helped my martial arts and self-defence training, but I need to do more running to keep up with you, Chloe."

Thabiti watched Chloe shake her head before securing her long blonde hair in a ponytail. They'd all settled in Nanyuki earlier in the year. He and Pearl had moved with their Ma from Nairobi, but Chloe had relocated from the UK.

Her husband Dan had left the British army and obtained a job with a security company in Kenya, but he was based in the north and spent weeks at a time away from home.

Although Chloe was older than Pearl and himself, probably in her mid-thirties, she was slowly becoming a close friend. And she was helping Pearl continue to recover from the depression she suffered after their mother's death.

As he reached into his rucksack for the girls' water bottles, Chloe asked, "How's Marina?

When I last spoke to her, she seemed to be enjoying her voluntary work?"

Marina was a young Indian woman he was friendly with. They had temporarily managed a lodge in Borana Conservancy after Marina's father had tried to introduce her to an Indian man she thought he wanted her to marry.

She had made it clear to her parents that she wasn't interested in an arranged marriage and had jumped at the opportunity to work at Kakuma Refugee Camp in northern Kenya.

"I think so, although it's punishingly hot and the poverty is distressing. Pearl, have you heard from her recently?" he enquired, as he handed her a water bottle.

"Yes. She told me she's enjoyed teaching some of the younger children, and she's helping one of the refugees set up a small cafe." Pearl unscrewed the cap of her water bottle.

"I can't picture a cafe in a refugee camp. It sounds like a paradox," commented Chloe before she tipped back her head and took a long slug of water.

Thabiti sat down on a flat piece of rock at the edge of the clearing and looked out over Nanyuki, and the Laikipia plateau beyond. "This land once belonged to the Kikuyu tribe. All the way to Nyeri, and beyond to the far Aberdare Range." He looked across at the ridged silhouette of the Aberdares, which his tribe, the Kikuyu, thought resembled a drying cow hide.

He continued, "Our ancestors would have herded sheep, picked berries and gathered firewood in the shadow of their sacred Mount Kenya."

Chloe wiped her mouth and asked, "Why is the mountain sacred?"

Pearl replied, "Because the Kikuyu believe that Ngai, the supreme God and creator of all things, descends with the clouds and sits on Mount Kenya."

"And did your family have land here?" Chloe asked.

Pearl looked across at Thabiti and shrugged.

Thabiti replied, "I believe so, but like most Kikuyu land the colonial British treated it as unoccupied, and claimed it as Crown Land. They ignored our tribal tenure system and redistributed it amongst the European and South African settlers in the early 1900s."

He listened to the chatter of birds in the trees at the edge of the clearing, before continuing, "I've been looking though Ma's accounts and she had steadily been selling land for housing. One piece was even sold to a group developing a shopping mall. I remember her telling me that grandfather refused to accept land as gift, in return for political allegiance, but from the records I've seen, he bought up small plots in villages outside the capital. And they've now been swallowed up as Nairobi has expanded."

Pearl sat down next to Thabiti and said, "I heard there are plans for a new shopping mall in Nanyuki."

"On the road leading out into Laikipia. But the rents are high, so it'll probably be mostly chain stores and mobile phone shops. I doubt many independent retailers will be interested."

Chloe stood on the edge of the rock and said, "That's a shame. I really miss not being able to buy quality clothes locally, and I'd love to see a specialist food shop."

"I wouldn't mind opening a clothes shop." admitted Pearl.

Thabiti's stomach clenched. "I'd hate working in a shop. All those people." He'd always felt anxious amongst groups of people, particularly strangers.

"That's why you have Marina. She was amazing running the lodge in Borana." Chloe stepped back from the edge, placed her leg on a large boulder and stretched.

"Da, sorry, Reggie, as he insists we call him, wants to invest in a shop in Nanyuki," announced Pearl.

Thabiti clenched his hands. He'd caught his father snooping around his room yesterday, even after he'd finally plucked up the courage to tell him to move out of the main house, into the guest cottage. He'd have to change the lock on his bedroom door.

"Thabiti." Pearl raised her voice.

He looked round at her.

"There you are. Chloe asked what you thought of Reggie's business proposal."

He stood up and faced Chloe. "I think he has the right idea. Many of the people moving to Nanyuki will need quality furnishings and a greater variety of household items than are currently available. But, ..."

Pearl jumped to her feet. "But what does he know about interior design and where is he sourcing his stock? And of course he kept dropping hints about looking for investors for his new venture. I finally told him that if he wanted money from us, it would be a loan from our trust fund, to be paid back with interest."

"Let's hope he makes a success of it," declared Chloe.

Thabiti clipped his cycle helmet on and shook his head. "No, he's up to something. A leopard doesn't change its spots."

CHAPTER FIVE

The following day Rose scratched her head as Thabiti showed her the tiny digits on the removable panel from her internet Wi-Fi router.

"They're so small I can't even read them with my glasses on." She picked up her iPad, "And I've found where to connect to the Wi-Fi on this, but how do I know which one to use?"

"Come with me," instructed Thabiti.

They walked out onto the covered patio and Thabiti reached for the pen and paper he'd left on Rose's wooden dining table. "I'll write everything down for you." He wrote 'Rose's Wi-

Fi' and underneath it a series of letters and numbers. "The internet connection should be easy to remember and underneath it I've written the password."

"Thank you," said Rose.

"And I'll visit Mr Obado's garage later. I'll buy a new air con filter for your Land Rover, and ask him about selling Craig's Subaru. As for your leaking roof, I'll need time to think about the best way to repair it. At least there's no rain forecast for the next few weeks."

"I am grateful," admitted Rose. "I thought I was prepared to tackle all the tasks Craig used to take care of, but clearly I was wrong."

"It's no trouble, especially after all the support you and Craig gave me."

Just then, Rose's phone rang.

Thabiti returned inside with the Wi-Fi panel as Rose answered the call. "Habari, Dr Emma. Do you need help treating a patient?"

"Rose, Habari. No, I've an appointment to view a property and wondered if you wanted to join me?"

"Yes, of course. Where and when?"

"In thirty minutes. Head out of Nanyuki towards Nairobi, and turn right onto the Ol Pejeta road. Then take the first right and it's house number five."

"I'll see you there. This is rather exciting." Rose put her phone away.

"What's exciting?" asked Thabiti emerging from the house.

"I'm viewing potential new veterinary premises with Dr Emma. Are you going home?" She picked up the paper and pen from the table.

"No, I've a meeting about an expedition onto the Aberdare Range."

Rose's eyes widened. "I didn't think you were into trekking and sleeping rough."

Thabiti slowly smiled. "I'm not. And it's only a day trip. The organisers want me to film and record their findings."

"And what are they looking for?"

"The remains of a World War II aeroplane. The leader of the expedition, Pete Stephenson, found wreckage of a Blenheim bomber three years ago, but there wasn't enough to identify it. Just some pieces of the undercarriage and rusty gears scattered around. But there's been a fire on the moorland above the Aberdare Forest, and rumours that more wreckage has appeared. Anyway, I'd better go or I'll be late."

CHAPTER SIX

Rose turned off a recently tarmacked section of road, leading to Ol Pejeta conservancy, onto a rutted track. She peered at the numbers attached to metal gates which protected the properties behind them. She discovered number five a hundred metres along the track, on the right-hand side, and turned into the drive through the open gates.

Dr Emma was talking to an African lady outside the front door of a large house. The lady was in her late thirties and looked professional with a white shirt and neat navy and white striped skirt.

"Habari Rose, thanks for coming. Isn't this terrific?" Dr Emma beamed at her.

Rose looked up at the property and her heart sank. It was an irregular shaped two storey house which would not lend itself well to a veterinary practice. And she observed that its concrete and painted render walls were dull and weeds grew in place of flowers by the door, and through the sparse gravel on the driveway. But she did not want to dampen Dr Emma's enthusiasm.

Still smiling Dr Emma said, "Can I introduce you to Hellen Newton who's set up the Nanyuki office of Jengo Real Estate."

Rose's reply was cut off as a shiny green Range Rover sped through the gates and braked sharply, scattering gravel and dust.

A smartly dressed man in a navy blazer emerged and eyed Rose's battered Land Rover Defender suspiciously. He called, "Hellen, a word."

Hellen walked with the man to the far end of the drive. He was talking, and gesticulating with his arms, whilst Hellen listened.

Suddenly Hellen cried, "But that's not possible."

The man shook his head and continued as Hellen's shoulders slumped and her arms hung limply by her side.

Rose turned to Dr Emma, whose head was tilted to one side. "Who's that man? He appears to be giving your real estate agent a hard time."

Dr Emma looked at Rose and wrinkled her nose. "That's Fergus Peacock. He's a Nairobi-based lawyer. Hellen said we were waiting for the owner to bring the keys, so I presume that's him. But surely he's not berating her about the viewing, we haven't even started yet."

Fergus Peacock turned and walked towards the house.

Hellen remained still for several seconds before squaring her shoulders and following Fergus. She reached Rose and Dr Emma, swallowed and announced in a hoarse voice, "Fergus, these are the vets who are interested in this property for their veterinary practice."

Rose looked at Fergus. If Hellen was introducing them, it was unlikely their previous discussion had been about the viewing.

"Are you locals?" Fergus scowled.

Dr Emma stepped forward and despite having to look up at Fergus she declared, "I'm Dr Emma, and together with my colleague, Mama Rose, I've been running Nanyuki's only veterinary practice for over ten years." She raised her eyebrows and Rose half-expected her to add, "Do you have a problem with that?" But instead Dr Emma gave him a crooked smile.

He coughed, looked over Dr Emma's shoulder to Hellen and held up a set of keys. "Shall we go in?"

Hellen led them through the front door into a spacious entrance hall. Looking around, she said in an upbeat tone, "This would make an excellent waiting area." She crossed the hall and opened a door on the far side. Stepping through, she commented, "And you could meet and examine your patients in here."

"It is a rather grand building," Fergus Peacock drawled, "But I do recognise the need for upmarket veterinary premises in Nanyuki."

Rose peered into the room Hellen had suggested as the examination room and didn't think it was grand at all. The lime green paint was peeling from the walls and there was a brown stain on the off-white ceiling.

Both could be fixed with fresh coats of paint, but she doubted Dr Emma wanted to start repairing the damaged parquet flooring. And there was a stale smell of sweat and onions.

She followed at the back of the group as Hellen gamely continued her tour, whilst Fergus added unhelpful comments about the non-existent virtues of the property.

On the first floor, he said, "And this area would make extremely comfortable living quarters, although it's probably larger than you're used to."

Dr Emma folded her arms across her chest.

Rose glanced out of a corridor window and thought she recognised the rear of a three-storey building on the other side of the fence. She shifted her head from side to side as she considered it. Of course, the road to this house ran parallel with the main Nanyuki highway and the building she was looking at was a nightclub which had recently opened.

According to local media, there had been numerous complaints about loud music playing until six or seven o'clock in the morning.

She turned, and feeling unusually mischievous said, "I'm surprised the British army aren't interested in such a large house. This is the type of property they usually snap up."

Fergus stopped speaking abruptly and his face coloured. He appeared flustered as he remarked, "I, we, were going to approach them next, but I thought I would offer it to you first."

Dr Emma joined Rose at the window and caught her breath as she looked out. Turning back to Fergus, her eyes narrowed as she demanded, "Are you sure they haven't already turned you down?" She took a step forward, "Since we are behind Stripes nightclub."

Hellen's shoulders hunched and she looked down at the scuffed floor.

Fergus stood rigid and declared, "If you don't want it, that's fine. I've changed my mind Hellen. I don't want a lot of sick animals cluttering up my property. These women can find somewhere else for their veterinary practice." He turned and stalked away.

As he reached the top of the stairs, Dr Emma burst out laughing. Rose smiled indulgently as they followed Fergus out of the house.

CHAPTER SEVEN

O utside the house there was no sign of Fergus Peacock or his Range Rover. Hellen Newton locked the front door as Dr Emma's mobile phone rang.

She answered it and listened for a minute before saying, "I'll be back at the pharmacy in five minutes." She turned to Rose and explained, "I've a patient waiting for me. Would you mind giving Hellen a lift back to Dormans?"

"Of course not," replied Rose as she fished her keys out of her trouser pocket.

Hellen shook Dr Emma's hand. "I'm sorry this property was such a disappointment. Fergus made out that it was far better than it is, and he didn't mention the night club. If you're happy, I'll continue to look around, although I suspect most property deals in Nanyuki are done through word of mouth."

Rose replied, "I think that's a fair assumption. You have to become involved in the local community before people start to trust you."

As Hellen climbed into the passenger seat of Rose's Defender, she asked, "Are you a member of the East Africa Women's League?"

"Yes, I am." Rose turned the key in the ignition.

"Someone suggested it as a good place to meet influential local residents."

Rose laughed, "It certainly is if you want to approach the lion head on."

Hellen looked out of the car window as they bumped along the track towards the Ol Pejeta Road. She turned back to Rose and asked, "Are you going to Thursday's meeting?"

"I'm not sure. Why? Do you want someone to go with you?"

"I've heard the members are an intimidating bunch."

Rose chuckled. "You've been speaking to Dr Emma. We're not all that bad, and the lunch is fantastic."

She searched for a gap in the traffic and pulled out behind a boda boda as she headed towards the main Nanyuki highway. Did she want to attend Thursday's meeting?

The members were her friends, and many had been for countless years. They understood grief having lost husbands, brothers, sisters and even children. And their sympathy would be genuine as several had worked with Craig on his various committees.

In a subdued voice she explained, "My husband, Craig, died a few weeks ago so I haven't felt like meeting people. I think the real reason Dr Emma invited me to view the property today was to get me away from my house."

"So will you introduce me to the members on Thursday?" Hellen rubbed her arm.

"Is meeting them important to you?"

"Succeeding in my job is, and for that, as you said, I need to become involved with the local community. It seems like a sensible place to start."

At the junction with the main Nanyuki highway, Rose waited for a tourist Land Cruiser to pull out in front of her. It probably was time she left the comfort and security of her house and began to mingle with people again. Even in sleepy Nanyuki life continued, and if she wasn't careful she'd be left behind.

She turned to Hellen and said, "Why not. Let's face the members of the Women's League together. But you'll need to bring a dish of food for lunch."

CHAPTER EIGHT

Rose found an empty parking space outside the complex that housed Dormans coffee shop, a gift shop and a number of offices. It was one of these offices that Jengo Real Estate occupied.

Hellen rubbed her hands down her skirt and said, "Thank you for the lift. Can I buy you a coffee?"

Rose hesitated and peered through the windscreen at the complex's metal arched entrance into the courtyard beyond. Two people sat at a table and a lone business man occupied another, eating a late breakfast or early lunch.

Her mouth was dry and she was relieved it wasn't busy. "Yes, I would like that, although I prefer tea to coffee," replied Rose.

"Mama Rose," a surprised sounding Thabiti greeted her as she and Hellen walked through the entrance archway. He was sitting at a circular picnic table, shaded by a canvas umbrella, to the right of the entrance. "Are you joining me for a drink?"

"Well …"

"Hellen," a dark-haired European man with a podgy face called. "Where have you been? Come and join us for coffee?" He was sitting with an attractive fair-haired man, with a tanned face and chiselled jawline.

Hellen turned to Rose and said, "Sorry, that's my husband, Alex. Do you mind?"

"Not at all. I'll keep Thabiti company."

"I'll still buy you that drink. Any particular tea? And do you take it with milk or lemon?"

"Kericho Gold, with milk, please,"

Hellen left in search of a waiter and Rose sat down opposite Thabiti. The complex was surrounded by a metre-high concrete wall, above which green-leafed plants clung to a wooden trellis. They were covered in a fine layer of dust thrown up by passing traffic.

Hellen returned and called across to her husband, "I'll be back in a minute. I just need to check my messages and emails."

Thabiti folded the newspaper he had been reading, leaned forward and murmured, "Who's that?"

"Hellen Newton. She's the one who showed Dr Emma and me around the property today. She's set up the new Jengo Real Estate office."

Thabiti's eyes followed Hellen's retreating back. "And was it any good?"

"No, it was dreadful, although nothing a lick of paint and some TLC couldn't take care of. It belongs to a Nairobi-based lawyer."

She lowered her voice and whispered, "I think he bought it believing the British army would pay him a huge rent. But that new nightclub has opened behind it, and there's no way the army families would live there and put up with the noise. He was pretty angry when he left us."

At the nearby table she heard the fair-haired man ask, "So, what about it? Are you in on the bet?"

Alex Newton glanced towards the door his wife had disappeared through. He turned back to his companion and in a strained voice replied, "No, Guy. I've given up my share in Desert Rose, and with her the gambling. You and Fergus can do what you like, but you're on your own. Besides, Hellen would kill me if she knew. You know we moved up to Nanyuki to make a fresh start."

Thabiti waved his newspaper in front of Rose. "Hello, are you with me?"

Rose turned back to him. "Sorry, my attention wandered."

Thabiti raised his eyebrows.

Hurriedly Rose asked, "Did you meet your plane hunters?"

Thabiti's eyes sparkled as he confided, "We're going next week. We'll stay at the Outspan Hotel in Nyeri on Thursday night, and leave before daybreak on Friday morning. We'll drive through the Aberdare Forest as far as the moorland and then continue on foot to the crash site."

Hellen joined her husband and the fair-haired man, Guy, at the adjacent table as a waiter brought Rose her tea.

A youthful looking European man with light, almost white, curly hair, which flopped over his face, hovered beside Thabiti.

Rose picked up Thabiti's newspaper and stared at the headlines and accompanying photo of two men in a field shaking hands.

The young man said in a distracted tone, "Good to meet you, Thabiti. I'll see you next week then." He looked towards the far table and called, "Is Becky joining you?"

Guy replied, "No. She and Eloise have gone to Nyeri, to visit Roho House."

The young man's fists clenched, and he muttered, almost to himself, "Maybe I'll catch her tomorrow." He turned and left the complex through the metal archway.

Rose poured hot water over her tea bag and asked, "Who was that?"

"Otto someone," replied Thabiti. "He's joining the expedition next week."

Rose's brow wrinkled as she stirred milk into her tea. "He doesn't look as if he'd be interested in a World War II plane wreckage."

"He's not. He's searching for a light aircraft which disappeared over the Aberdares nearly ten years ago." Thabiti tapped the newspaper. "So what do you think of the proposal to build a new brewery in Nyeri?"

"I suppose it brings employment opportunities, and competition for East African Breweries can only be a good thing. But why does it interest you?" Rose gratefully sipped her tea.

Thabiti sat up. "Tucan Breweries, the new company, is implementing environmental sustainability practices. For instance, it plans a mini-hydroelectric scheme to power its brewery, as well as an adjacent tea farm and nearby dwellings. And its waste disposal includes a hydroponics system for growing vegetables for its staff."

Thabiti picked at a corner of the newspaper. "I hope it goes ahead. There were plans for a similar venture ten years ago, but the brewery pulled out. Something to do with sacred land and a curse, if you can believe that."

Rose drank more tea and heard Hellen apologise to her husband. "Sorry I left before breakfast. I had my first viewing this morning."

Alex placed a hand on her arm and asked, "How did it go?"

She looked down at the table and replied, "Abysmally. Fergus hadn't even bothered to clean the property. And the ceilings were stained and paint was peeling off the walls."

"I thought he bought that place so he could rent it to the British Army at an astronomical price."

Hellen sighed, "He did, but they won't touch it with a nightclub next door."

CHAPTER NINE

For the second morning in a row, Rose walked through the metal entrance arch of the complex which housed Dormans coffee shop and Jengo Real Estate. She stopped in surprise.

Two vertical banners, proclaiming 'The Great Grevy's Rally', were positioned either side of the large wooden table in front of her, and a small queue of people chatted quietly. She looked across to her left, but the corner table where she and Chloe usually sat was occupied by other customers.

"Rose," Chloe called.

Rose turned and found Chloe sitting to the right of the entrance, at the same table Thabiti had occupied the previous day.

She joined Chloe, who stood up and air-kissed her on both cheeks. "I'm so glad you've come. It feels like ages since I last saw you, although it's probably only been a couple of weeks."

Rose sat down and looked around uncertainly. "I'm not sure I would have come if I'd realised how many people would be here. What's going on?"

"Gabriel Baker, who you may remember from the Giants Club Summit. Well he's taking entries today for the Great Grevy's Rally. Besides meeting you, it's the reason I'm here. Dan's asked me to enter a company team."

Rose turned towards the registration table and spotted Gabriel Baker with his shoulder-length brown hair. As she turned back towards Chloe her attention was caught by a young man with very fair, curly hair. Thabiti had told her his name was Otto. He was joined by a teenage girl whose long, lean legs were accentuated by a pair of tight-fitting red jodhpurs.

Chloe ordered a cappuccino for herself and tea for Rose. She tapped the menu before admitting, "I was going to ask if you needed any help sorting through Craig's things, but I never felt the time was right."

Rose smiled warmly. "It's kind of you to think about it but don't worry, Kipto helped me. We've given clothes to the homeless men's shelter and to Huduma Hospice. And Samwell and Kipto kept a few items for themselves and their families. And how have you been? How are things with Dan?"

Chloe examined her nails and replied, "We're back on an even keel, and I still see the counsellor you recommended once a week, which helps." She looked up as their drinks arrived.

As the waiter departed she disclosed, "To tell you the truth, I'm rather bored. Now the house is the way I want it, and I'm no longer training for the Lewa marathon, I don't have anything meaningful to do. No challenges of any sort."

She raised a hand and bit her nail. Without looking at Rose she confessed, "It would be different if I had kids, but then you know all about that."

"So you're still struggling?"

"It doesn't help when Dan is away so much, but I am seeing a new specialist in Nairobi in a couple of weeks. Maybe she can help. But in the meantime, I'm not sure what to do with myself."

"You could come to the East Africa Women's League meeting tomorrow."

"Isn't that rather fuddy-duddy? I imagine the members sitting around swapping jam recipes and talking about knitting?"

Rose grinned and her chest heaved with suppressed laughter as she imagined her fellow members, bent double over their knitting or crochet, as they mumbled at each other through toothless gums. "Can you really see me doing that?"

Chloe smiled ruefully as she stirred her cappuccino. "OK, not you. But the other members."

"Put it this way, we had a visitor from the UK a few months ago who was shocked by the language of some members, and the number of empty wine bottles at the end of the meeting."

Still grinning, Rose lifted her cup and sipped her tea. Then she said, "Hellen Newton, the new real estate agent, has asked me to introduce her to the members at tomorrow's meeting, so why don't you join us?"

Chloe wiped frothy milk from her top lip and replied, "I can hardly refuse since I've just complained about being bored. When and where is the meeting?"

"It's being held at a member's house, just beyond Cape Chestnut restaurant. But I was going to suggest to Hellen that I met her here."

Out of the corner of her eye, she noted Otto jump to his feet as he cried, "Becky."

Rose looked towards the entrance arch as two fair-haired women entered. The older one had a handsome but lined face, and she wore her hair up in a loose bun. The younger woman looked more carefree and her long fair locks hung loose around her shoulders.

The older woman leaned towards the younger and murmured, "You better see what Otto wants. I'll join the registration line for the Grevy's Rally."

Rose's gaze followed the younger woman as she joined Otto and said, "It's been lovely catching up with you again. But I'm only in Kenya for a few more weeks and I still have other people to see, and some family matters to sort out."

"I hear you visited Roho House yesterday? I was telling Sophia," he indicated towards the teenage girl, "how your father taught me to play polo on the front lawn at Roho."

The woman tucked a strand of fair hair behind her ear. "We had some great times there growing up. That's why I wanted to see it again before we decide what to do with it."

"Becky. You're not going to sell it are you?" Otto raised his voice.

Becky shrugged. "My life is in the UK now, and my fiancé and I have bought our own house. Eloise and Guy don't want to live in Nyeri and the tenants have neglected it. Selling seems the most sensible option."

Otto raised his arm towards Becky. "But what about me? About us?"

Becky stepped back. "I've already explained. There is no us. There never has been …"

"But I thought, everyone did, that you'd come back to Kenya and we'd get married," interjected Otto.

The corners of Becky's mouth wrinkled and her nose twitched. "No, they didn't. We were childhood friends but now I've moved on. And so have you." She glanced towards Sophia.

Otto stepped forward, "There's nothing going on between Sophia and me. I promised her father I'd show her around. He's bought a plot at Timau, next to the new polo ground." Otto's voice had a petulant tone.

Becky raised her eyebrows. "Sure, whatever you say. Now, I must get back to Eloise. It's been fantastic catching up, but it's time to say goodbye."

Otto grabbed her arm. "You can't mean that."

Becky gasped and tried to pull her arm away. "Otto, you're hurting me."

Hellen Newton appeared and joined Otto and Becky. She asked in a concerned voice, "Becky, are you all right?"

Otto released Becky, and she rubbed her arm. "I'm fine, thank you, Hellen."

Hellen turned and walked towards Rose, blocking her view of the couple, but she heard Otto whisper in a hoarse voice, "I'm not giving up that easily. You and I were meant to be together. If I can't have you, then I won't let anyone else."

"Habari, Rose," Hellen said brightly, breaking Rose's concentration. She slid onto the seat beside Rose and declared, "About tomorrow's meeting, I've been thinking that maybe I should wait a bit. Get to know some of the Nanyuki residents before I attend a Women's League meeting."

"That's a shame, I had invited Chloe to join us." Rose turned towards Chloe, but her seat was empty. "Chloe?" Rose repeated, wrinkling her brow.

"I'm here," Chloe said brightly as she sat down. "I went to register Dan's team for the Great

Grevy's rally whilst your attention was elsewhere." She put her hand over her mouth to try to hide her grin.

"Yes, well," stammered Rose. "I wanted to introduce you to Hellen Newton, who I told you wanted to come to the Women's League meeting tomorrow."

Chloe leaned forward and touched Hellen's arm and confided, "That's wonderful. I've been curious about the Women's League for ages. I thought they were a group of old women who sit around gossiping, but Rose assures me they're not."

"I said we don't sit around knitting and swapping jam recipes. There's plenty of gossip to go with the wine."

"Wine," remarked Hellen. "It doesn't sound so bad after all."

Rose clasped her hands together. "Excellent. I'll pick you both up here tomorrow at ten to twelve. And make sure you bring a dish for lunch."

CHAPTER TEN

Rose stood up, stretched her back and flexed her arthritic fingers. She was in her vegetable garden picking lettuce leaves for the Women's League lunch. Her daughter Heather had brought her a variety of seeds from the UK on her last visit, including a mixture of salad leaves.

Heather had arrived just in time to see and briefly speak with her father before he died. Rose suspected Craig had been hanging on to see his daughter as he passed away soon after their reunion. She sniffed and thought of Heather in the UK, busy with her own family.

She picked up her bowl of lettuce and returned to the kitchen. Kipto tapped the lid of an old metal biscuit tin. "I make cheesy bombs," she announced proudly.

Perplexed, Rose struggled to prise open the lid of the tin. When it finally lifted off, she looked inside and said gratefully, "Ah, cheese scones. And they smell wonderful. Thank you."

Kipto beamed.

Hellen Newton and Chloe were waiting at the entrance to the Dormans complex when Rose drew up in her battered red Land Rover and waved at them. Hellen carried a large wooden bowl covered in foil and Chloe an oval, china serving platter. Rose leaned over, opened the passenger door and called, "It might be a bit of a squeeze, but jump in."

"Thank you. Can you hold this for me?" asked Hellen, passing across the bowl.

Rose smelt the familiar aroma of feta and coriander samosas and her mouth watered. "They smell delicious."

As Hellen shuffled along the seat to make room for Chloe, she replied, "I hope they don't cool too much before lunch."

"We can ask our hostess if she can keep them warm. Are you in Chloe?" asked Rose.

Chloe shuffled and then slammed the door closed. "I am now."

Rose turned to Hellen, "It's not far, anyway."

Rose turned off the main Nanyuki highway onto the road leading to the Cottage Hospital. She branched right and followed the track past Cape Chestnut restaurant. Cars of varying colour, size and age were parked along the verge leading to a single-storey, wooden, colonial-style house.

"Is it always this busy?" asked Chloe.

"I suppose it is," replied Rose, as she parked in front of a wooden shed, whose padlocked door hung down at an angle on its rusty hinges.

Carrying their various lunch dishes, they entered the house and were greeted by Poppy Chambers. She wore her glasses on a beaded chain which hung in loops on either side of her face. "Rose Hardie," she muttered as she searched a sheet of paper on the table in front of her. She ticked off Rose's name and added, "And you've brought two guests."

"Have you already met Chloe Collins?" Rose asked as she touched Chloe's arm.

Poppy turned to Chloe. "We've not been introduced, but I've seen you around Nanyuki. Welcome to our meeting. Would you mind completing this form?" She handed Chloe a pen and paper.

Rose continued, "And this is Hellen Newton, who's set up Jengo Real Estate's Nanyuki office."

Poppy held out a hand. "Lovely to meet you. I've seen you in Podo School, in the car park, when I've been picking up my granddaughter."

Hellen confirmed, "My daughter, Mia, is a pupil and my son, Liam, will start pre-prep in the Autumn. What shall I do with these samosas?" She held up her bowl. "It would be best if they were kept warm."

"Did someone say samosas," asked a small, elderly lady with a bob of white hair.

"Ah, Dora," said Poppy. "Please can you help Chloe complete her registration form whilst I find Hellen somewhere warm for her samosas." As Poppy and Hellen walked into the adjoining room Rose heard Poppy ask, "So where are you living?"

"All done," said Chloe brightly. She held up the form and a thousand shilling note, which was her guest fee for the meeting and lunch.

"That's lovely. What wonderful hair you have," cooed Dora.

"Thank you, Dora," said Rose briskly as she took Chloe by the elbow and led her to an adjacent table where drinks were laid out. They both picked up glasses of white wine and continued down the corridor to a large and airy conservatory.

There was an abundance of greenery provided by palms, ornamental grasses and cacti. Attractive birds of paradise plants, desert roses and a variety of red, white and pink cyclamen provided splashes of colour.

Several rows of fold-up chairs had been arranged, facing the far end of the conservatory, in readiness for the formal part of the meeting, and a talk from a guest speaker.

"Rose." She was greeted warmly by Birdie Rawlinson, an old friend. "Come and join us, it's so lovely to see you."

"Hello, Birdie." Rose smiled and exchanged greetings with the group of women standing in the corner of the conservatory, by a door leading into the rear garden.

"We were just commenting on how well the yesterday-today-and-tomorrow is growing. You can smell its wonderful fragrance from here." Birdie turned to Rose and asked, "And how are you, my dear?"

Few people could get away with calling Rose 'dear' but Birdie was one of them. They were both in their mid-sixties and had grown up in Kenya, meeting regularly at polo matches, horse shows and holidays at Kenya's white-beached coast. Birdie's husband, Terry, and Craig had both worked as farm managers.

Rose placed her hand on Birdie's arm. "I'm OK. I just need time getting used to Craig not being around. But let me introduce you to Chloe."

Chloe shook hands with Birdie, and various other women who came forward to welcome her to the meeting.

Birdie looked at Chloe and asked, "Did you enter the Great Grevy's Rally yesterday?"

Chloe confessed, "Not for myself, but for my husband and his colleagues. Are you taking part?"

Birdie rubbed her chin and replied, "I'm not sure. I'm really too old for that sort of thing. But my oldest son and his family are doing their best to persuade me to join them. What about you, Rose?"

"Not this year."

The diminutive Dora hurried in, pulling a reluctant Hellen, and announced, "Everyone, say hello to Hellen."

Hellen leaned back and half-raised her hand as she said a hesitant, "Hi."

"Aren't you the new estate agent?" Birdie asked in a matter-of-fact tone. "We need someone in Nanyuki who can work out who owns what, and stop those in power grabbing any land they fancy."

"Birdie," a voice warned.

Hellen stepped forward, "I'm very happy to help you, and your friends and family, buy, sell or rent property. But I hope I won't get embroiled in any legal disputes."

Birdie shrugged her shoulders. "That's a shame. Now, did I see you talking to Eloise and Rebecca Munro the other day?"

"Do you mean Eloise Ramsey? And her sister Becky?" Asked Hellen, tilting her head to one side.

"Tall, attractive, fair-haired women. Their parents, God bless them, disappeared over the Aberdares, several years ago," responded Birdie.

"Poor Mick and Geraldine. Has someone found them?" Dora's lip trembled as she looked from Birdie to Hellen.

Birdie placed her hand on Dora's shoulder. "No, they and their plane are still missing."

Dora's eyes widened as she asked, "Their daughter married Edna's grandson, didn't she?"

Rose was trying to follow the meandering thread of the conversation. She turned to Hellen and said, "Only Eloise is married, isn't she? To your husband's friend, Guy, who was sitting with him in Dormans the day we viewed the property near the nightclub."

Hellen confirmed, "That's right, Guy Ramsey. He and my husband, Alex, are business partners."

"And Guy is the grandson of Edna, the artist who lives in Nairobi?" Rose asked, turning back to Birdie.

"He is," confirmed Birdie. "And she spoilt him rotten when he was growing up. I guess she was trying to make amends because his parents abandoned him. How his marriage to Eloise Munro is still intact, I've no idea. Edna was forever dripping poison against the Munros, convinced that Eloise's grandfather had swindled her out of her house and fortune."

"Well, she's right." Dora crossed her arms over her chest and looked defiant.

"Dora, we don't know that," said Birdie in a soothing voice. "Anyway, she's far better off in Nairobi than at Roho House."

Rose's attention was caught by Roho House. Hadn't Otto and Becky been discussing it in Dormans the previous day.

Dora was shaking. "It's cursed that land. Look what happened to Mick and Geraldine."

Rose heard Hellen mutter, "And rightly so." She looked across and noted Hellen's clenched fists and set expression. Now what had brought that on?

Her thoughts were interrupted as Poppy Chambers walked into the conservatory and announced, "Lunch is served."

CHAPTER ELEVEN

At lunchtime on Saturday, Rose drove into the car park of Bushman's Restaurant and found a space beside the white-painted concrete wall, which separated it from the restaurant's small garden.

She decided not to enter through the main building, but instead chose the bottom entrance via the garden. As she reached the gate, a voice called out, "Mama Rose." She stopped and turned.

"How are you?" said the concerned face of a small but fit-looking young African woman.

"Constable Wachira." Rose stopped and raised her hand as the younger woman was about to protest. "I know, I know, you prefer to be called Judy, especially since you're not wearing your uniform. But is a police officer ever completely off duty?"

"Probably not. And despite this being my day off, I've already had to secure a property after thieves broke in. The elderly owner, Mrs Sharpe, is in hospital." The young woman added in a disgusted tone.

Rose straightened up. "How awful. Winnie's a game old bird, but she's been selling anything of value since her husband died to pay her medical bills. I didn't think there was much left to take."

An image of Winnie Sharpe's small living room popped into Rose's mind, with a sofa covered by frayed tartan rugs and numerous cushions, to cover holes where the horsehair stuffing protruded.

"It was hard to tell what the thieves took," admitted the young constable. "The few items of jewellery she has left, and her small collection of silver-framed photographs, are with her in hospital. I think a couple of lamps are missing, as two shades had been discarded, and the linen cupboard was open with pillowcases and sheets strewn across the floor."

"I'd better pay her a visit and make sure she's not fretting. What about her staff?"

"There only seems to be an elderly man who lives next door. He checks on her several times a day when she's home. He's the one who alerted us to the break in."

The constable gently placed her hand on Rose's arm. "I hope this incident is a one-off but I have a feeling it might not be. And if the thieves are targeting elderly people, living on their own, you need to be careful." She let go of Rose's arm and enquired, "I haven't seen you since Craig's memorial. How are you managing?"

Rose looked past the young constable through the open gate. "I'm still getting used to him not being around. Sometimes I find myself turning towards his chair and I've half asked a question before I realise he's not there. But I'm trying to keep myself busy. Apart from the break-in, how have you been?"

"I'm fed up with traffic duty." Constable Wachira pinched her lips together before continuing, "Commissioner Akida keeps being called away and, each time he leaves, Sergeant Sebunya assigns me to traffic duty. I'm not sure why, as I refuse to take bribes, so he doesn't get his cut from me. It's OK when Inspector Kamau is around. I've accompanied him on a number of different cases and he's helping me prepare for my sergeant's exams."

"When are they?" Rose enquired. She hoped the young constable passed as she was intelligent, conscientious and fair.

"In less than two weeks, and I still have a lot to learn. I should really be studying now." She looked down at the gravel path.

"But instead you're meeting a certain young man?"

The younger woman coughed. "He's here for an interview." The man they were referring to was Sam Mwamba, and Rose was unsure why the attractive constable was embarrassed to admit they were in a relationship. She liked Sam who was a gentle giant of a man, although she would not want to be near him when when he was angry.

"What type of interview?" Rose asked, gesturing towards the restaurant entrance.

Constable Wachira dropped her voice, "For a job at Ol Pejeta Conservancy. They're looking for a new Director of Operations."

Rose and Constable Wachira walked into the garden of the Bushman's Restaurant and turned left towards the main outdoor seating area.

"I'll wait here," whispered Constable Wachira. "Ol Pejeta have borrowed Global Vista's office to conduct the interview."

Rose looked back down the garden. Beyond the gravel path was the Global Vista office, a gift shop, a wine shop and a beautician. In the far corner was a small studio, which could be hired out.

The door of the Global Vista office opened and a bald-headed man stepped out. He turned to the other occupants of the room and Rose heard him say, "Thank you for coming. We'll be in touch." He turned and rushed out of the bottom gate into the car park.

A large African man seemed to squeeze his way through the door. Sunlight glinted off his ear.

Rose turned to her companion and said, "I thought Sam's earring was just for one of his undercover jobs?"

Constable Wachira smiled and replied, "He's become rather fond of it. Although I am surprised he's wearing it to his interview."

A third man stepped out of the office, who Rose recognised as the lawyer, Fergus Peacock. He wore a neat-fitting grey suit with a maroon-coloured tie. As Rose watched, he clipped a pen to his breast pocket before shaking Sam's hand. He turned and strode briskly past her and she heard him hail, "Hellen, can I have a word?"

Sam joined Rose and put an arm around Constable Wachira, whose cheeks turned pink.

Rose asked, "How was your interview?"

"It's hard to tell," the large man drawled. "There are at least three other candidates. I know two of them are far better qualified than me, but I still might stand a chance. After a recent court case involving work permits, the conservancy are keen to employ a Kenyan citizen."

Rose placed a hand on his arm. "I'm sure you'd be great at the job. Especially with all your anti-poaching experience."

Sam was an officer of the Kenya Wildlife Service, but he'd recently been working for the Kenya Anti-Poaching Unit. Much of his work was undercover as the agency attempted to infiltrate poaching gangs and prevent them killing wild animals, particularly rhinos and elephants for their ivory horns and tusks.

"Are you meeting anyone?" Constable Wachira asked Rose.

"Yes, Chloe invited me for lunch with Thabiti and Pearl," she replied. "Would you like to join us?"

Sam looked across the outdoor restaurant area, and then down at Constable Wachira and said, "I'm not sure about lunch but how about a drink? I wouldn't mind a beer after that interrogation, and I've just seen Thabiti arrive."

Rose turned and found her way blocked by a woman with dark hair, in her late thirties or early forties, who emerged from the main restaurant and hailed a waiter. She held a clipboard against which she tapped her pen as she said to the waiter, "I've taken my tour group's order from the set menu you provided, but some of them have requested changes."

"Tessa," a man called.

The dark-haired woman looked up and her eyes narrowed. She called back, "Just a minute, Alex," and continued speaking to the waiter.

Rose stepped around them and heard the woman say, "Asante."

Alex Newton, with his dark hair and chubby face, peeled himself away from a group clustered around a table and smiled. He cried, "Tessa, this is wonderful, we haven't seen you for ages."

Behind her, Rose heard the dark-haired woman respond, "Well, you did move to Nanyuki."

"I know, but you're a tour guide, and I presume you pass through all the time on your trips between Nairobi and Samburu, or out onto the Laikipia Plateau."

Rose stopped and turned, finding herself drawn to the conversation. She heard Sam call, "Thabiti."

Tessa was the woman who had been speaking with the waiter, and she approached Alex tapping her pen against her clipboard. She wore her hair in a short bob, with a long fringe, and she had a purple scarf wrapped around her neck, under a branded polo shirt.

She said tartly, "I don't have the luxury of managing a business. I actually have to work for a living. And when I pass through, or stop in Nanyuki, I'm always surrounded by tourists who are clamouring for my attention."

Alex looked down at the floor.

Tessa continued in a scathing tone, "At least Hellen's trying to earn a living. I understand she's working for Jengo Real Estate, in their newly opened Nanyuki office. But what about you, Alex?" She sneered. "Rumour has it that the business, Dad's business, is in trouble."

Alex shuffled his feet.

"And I've heard you're looking for a cash injection as the banks won't extend your loans.

Have you really spent all Eloise's money which Guy invested in your safari business? This would never have happened if Dad had left the company to me." She spat the words of the final sentence.

Alex had a pained expression on his face as he raised his eyes to Tessa and said in a conciliatory tone, "I know I'm a constant disappointment to you, as I was to Dad. I've no idea why he left the business to me. After all, you were his favourite. But I think we've found an investor. And I promise, I will work hard and turn the business around. It's one of the reasons we moved to Nanyuki. To reduce our outgoings."

"And there are fewer temptations," Tessa quipped.

The tension was broken as a young girl, in a pink dress, ran across and hugged Tessa's legs. "Auntie Tessa. Will you play with me? Mummy's busy talking to a man." She whispered, "And he is making her sad."

CHAPTER TWELVE

Rose joined Chloe, Thabiti, Sam and Constable Wachira who were standing beside a table at the edge of the outdoor eating area. A large, fluffy grey cat rolled contentedly in the nearby flowerbed.

"Rose, what would you like to drink?" asked Sam.

"A fresh lime juice with soda water, please."

"So that's two Tuskers, a gin and tonic and lime juice with soda water."

Sam left to order drinks from the bar inside the restaurant as the others sat down.

"Is Pearl joining us?" asked Chloe.

"Shortly. She's working out in the studio at the bottom of the garden," replied Thabiti.

Rose glanced towards the studio but her attention was caught by Hellen Newton who was writing a cheque. She tore it from her chequebook and thrust it at Fergus Peacock who removed it from her hand with a slow, deliberate movement. Throwing her pen and chequebook on the table, Hellen sat down beside a toddler who was settled in a high chair, moving a toy car around the front tray.

Fergus stalked around the table and joined the fair-haired Guy Ramsey.

Rose turned back to her companions as Constable Wachira, picking at the sleeve of her shirt, muttered, "Excuse me, I'm just going to find the ladies."

"It's over there," replied Chloe, pointing to a single-storey building behind them.

Rose looked across at Thabiti and asked, "How's your father?"

Thabiti rolled his eyes. "He's very pleased with himself as we've agreed to lend him fifty thousand shillings to invest in a homeware duka in Nanyuki."

"That sounds like an interesting venture." Rose's eye was drawn to Hellen Newton, whose toddler was now wailing. Hellen opened a bag of snacks and gave one to the child, who immediately calmed down.

Beyond Hellen, Rose recognised Becky Munro and the lady who'd entered Dormans with her, who Rose presumed was her older sister Eloise. The two women certainly had a strong family resemblance.

The young girl in the pink dress approached Becky, and taking her arms they began to dance. They both laughed as they swayed to-and-fro, drawing the attention of those around them.

Chloe said, "Rose," but she barely registered the remark. She was transfixed by the pink-clad girl, who was now spinning in a circle whilst Becky, her dancing partner, slowly moved her arms and body from side to side.

"Steady Mia," called Alex, who was standing next to his wife. Beside him Tessa, the tour guide, clapped.

"Rose, are you going to join us?" Thabiti asked, as he tapped the table.

Rose shook her head and turned to him, "Sorry. That young girl dancing completely mesmerised …"

She was cut off by a scream and gasps from the crowd of diners.

The girl stopped spinning and ran towards Becky, her dancing partner, who had fallen to the ground. Rose heard a glass shatter and watched Sam race across to the prostrate figure. Without thinking, she stood and rushed to join him.

Alex dragged the young girl back as she enquired innocently, "What's wrong with Becky?"

Rose bent over the figure, whose limbs were jerking, and said to Sam, "She's having a seizure."

As Sam lifted Becky, trying to avoid her flailing arms, Rose asked the gathered group, "Does she have epilepsy? Or a history of seizures?"

"No, nothing we're aware of," answered Guy. He leaned forward as Sam carried Becky past and said, in a fascinated tone, "Her lips are blue."

Rose followed Sam, who laid Becky on the grass, and observed, "This doesn't look good, her breathing must be affected." She knelt beside the still figure and asked, "Becky, can you hear me?"

Becky opened her eyes and stared at Rose. She whispered, "Help me," before closing her eyes again. Her twitching arms stilled.

"Becky. Becky," Rose repeated, but she didn't receive a response. "I think she's unconscious. Can you help me?"

Sam rolled Becky over and Rose arranged her legs into the recovery position. As she moved Becky's arms she noticed a small cut, with dark edges, was bleeding. She must have injured herself when she fell to the paved floor. Becky lay limply on the ground, giving only the occasional jerk.

As Rose lifted Becky's wrist, she heard Constable Wachira say, "I've called the Cottage Hospital, and Dr Farrukh is on her way."

"She'd better hurry. This pulse is far too slow. We're losing her."

Rose watched helplessly as Becky's body stilled and seemed to deflate in front of her. She knew she was dead.

Rose drew in a deep breath and looked up as a solitary cloud covered the sun. Why hadn't she been able to prevent this vibrant young woman from dying? She felt like screaming. Was she screaming? Suddenly she became aware of the cacophony of noise around her. Gasps, cries and loud conversations from the other diners.

Rose looked up at the handsome face of the woman she thought was Becky's sister, who whispered, "Is she dead?"

Rose could only nod.

"No!" wailed the woman dropping to her knees and hugging the limp figure on the ground.

CHAPTER THIRTEEN

G uy, who was as white as a marble statue, wrapped his arms around the woman who was cradling the dead body.

"Come away, Eloise. There's nothing you can do for her now."

Eloise stood and buried her head in Guy's chest. Rose heard her say, in between sobs which racked her entire body, "I don't understand, how can she be dead?"

Guy rubbed her back.

Rose stood, brushing grass from her knees, as she heard voices shout, "What happened? Is she dead?"

Sam appeared beside her with a white tablecloth. "Poor woman, she deserves some privacy." He draped the cloth over Becky's body.

At the far end of the garden, by the now closed Global Vista office, Constable Wachira was speaking into her phone.

When she rejoined Sam and Rose she said, "Commissioner Akida has just returned from Nairobi so he'll be with us shortly. In the meantime, he's asked me to gather the names and addresses of all the witnesses."

She looked around the packed external seating area, and the people crowded into the doorway of the restaurant, and pressed her lips together. "I'd better get started."

She removed a small notebook from her trouser pocket and patted her other pockets. "No pen," she muttered as she walked towards the group who had been with Becky.

She picked a pen up from the table but threw it down again. A passing waiter handed her his biro and placed the discarded pen on his tray, between the glasses he carried.

"Sir, your drinks," he said to Sam.

Sam turned to Rose and apologised, "I'm sorry, I dropped your glass of juice when I rushed to help the fallen woman."

Rose placed a hand on his arm and replied, "Don't worry, I think I need something stronger than lime juice after what's happened."

Sam looked at the drinks and Rose followed his gaze. "What about Chloe's gin and tonic? I can order her a new one?"

"Thank you." Rose picked up the glass which knocked against the discarded pen. No wonder it didn't work. Both ends were missing and an elastic band was wrapped around it. She took a sip of the gin and tonic and grimaced at its sour taste. But at least she felt more alert.

Sam took a bottle of Tusker and instructed the waiter, "Please take the remaining drinks to the far table," he indicated with his bottle of beer, "And can you pour a fresh gin and tonic for the blonde-haired lady."

When the waiter had left, Sam and Rose stared down at the tablecloth which covered Becky's body.

"What a waste," remarked Rose before taking another sip of her drink. "Death comes to us all. I know that better than most. But Craig was in his seventies and had experienced a full and varied life. This young woman was just beginning hers."

"Oh dear, am I too late?" asked an earnest-looking Indian woman who approached them from the direction of the garden gate.

"Doctor, it's good of you to come, but I'm afraid the woman died very quickly. Mama Rose did what she could, but I doubt anyone could have stopped her dying," replied Sam.

"Is this her body?" asked Dr Farrukh, gesturing towards the cloth covered mound on the ground.

"Yes," confirmed Sam. "I hope you don't mind, but we wanted to give her some privacy away from prying eyes." He indicated towards the restaurant's diners. A number of them had turned to watch the doctor's arrival.

"Tell me what happened whilst I examine the body." Dr Farrukh crouched on the ground.

Rose explained the events including the collapse of the dead woman, her convulsions, slowing heart rate, unconsciousness and death.

Sam left Rose and the doctor and she heard him say, "Commissioner Akida. This way. Dr Farrukh has arrived and is examining the body."

The commissioner removed his dark-blue peaked cap, with its row of twisted silver oak leaves, and clasped it in front of him as he stared down at the dead woman.

"She looks like a young girl. There's a touch of innocence about her." He pulled a spotted handkerchief from his trouser pocket and turned away as he blew his nose. He replaced his cap and asked, "Dr Farrukh, what can you tell us?"

The doctor laid the woman's head back on the ground, replaced the cloth and stood up. Removing her white latex gloves, she said, "Heart attack, I would say, after hearing Rose's account and examining the body. But I can't say what caused it. Who's her next of kin?"

Sam answered, "She has a sister, who is here but is understandably distressed."

A phone rang and Dr Farrukh murmured, "Excuse me."

"Who is the dead woman? Should I recognise her?" enquired the commissioner.

"She's called Becky, Becky Munro, I believe, and she lives in the UK," responded Rose.

Sam looked at her intently and remarked, "And you discovered that in the last few minutes."

"No," Rose pursed her lips. "But she and her family have been the subject of a number of discussions recently."

Dr Farrukh rejoined them. "I'm sorry but I'm needed elsewhere. Did you say her sister is here?"

"Yes," confirmed Sam.

"Well, there are a few things we need her to confirm. Will you walk with me to my car, Rose, so I can discuss them with you?"

Rose looked towards Commissioner Akida who nodded his acceptance and she fell into step with Dr Farrukh.

"I don't believe the woman is local," Dr Farrukh commented. "I've never treated her."

"No, she's not," admitted Rose.

"So we need to establish if she had a heart problem. Or any other condition such as an underactive thyroid, imbalance of chemicals, or sleep apnoea. Also, if she'd suffered from any inflammatory diseases, such as rheumatic fever or lupus, which could have damaged her heart. Find out what, if any, medication she was on, or had been taking recently."

They stopped by an old-style, silver Mercedes-Benz and Dr Farrukh unlocked the driver's side door.

"I'll leave it with you. But feel free to call me later to discuss anything you find out." She climbed into her car and reversed out of the car park.

CHAPTER FOURTEEN

Rose joined Commissioner Akida and Sam, who were still standing by the covered body.

"We need the sister, as next of kin, to formally identify the body," stated the commissioner.

"And we need to ask her about Becky's medical history to establish what caused her heart attack," added Rose.

Chloe, Thabiti and Pearl joined them.

"We wondered if we could help," said Chloe, who averted her eyes from the tablecloth on the ground.

"What we need," the commissioner said, and his forehead wrinkled as he looked at the crowded restaurant, "is somewhere out of this sun to interview the witnesses."

"What about the studio?" suggested Pearl.

He turned to her with raised eyebrows. "The what?"

She pointed to the corner of the building at the bottom of the small garden. "It's a fitness studio, but we could move a table and some chairs inside. It's cool and quiet once the doors are closed." She held aloft a set of keys on a beaded key ring. "And I still have the keys."

Pearl, Chloe and Thabiti busied themselves carrying furniture into the studio.

"Which one is the sister?" asked Commissioner Akida.

Rose looked across at the external seating area of the restaurant. She watched Constable Wachira speak to the occupants of one of the tables. She wrote some notes in her notebook before moving on to the adjacent table. The group from the first table stood and gathered their possessions. Now the drama was over people were beginning to leave.

Tessa, the tour guide, strode towards them with a set expression.

"Are you in charge?" she demanded of Commissioner Akida.

He puffed out his chest and replied firmly, "I am."

She tapped her fingers against her clipboard. "Your constable told me I can't leave until you've interviewed me. But I'm in charge of a group of American tourists, and they have to be at Nanyuki Airstrip in forty-five minutes, at the latest, to catch their flight to Nairobi. Believe me, you don't want this lot on your hands overnight."

The commissioner leaned towards Tessa and enquired, "And how are you related to the deceased?"

"I'm not. In fact, I wasn't part of her group, but my brother was and he wanted to speak to me. And I wanted to see my niece." Her face softened.

Thabiti, Pearl and Chloe returned.

"All done," said Thabiti.

"And I've left the keys in the door," added Pearl. "Can you hand them back at the bar when you've finished?"

Commissioner Akida tapped the ends of his fingers together. "We need to formally identify the body before we conduct any interviews. Do you know the deceased woman's sister?"

"Eloise, yes," replied Tessa.

"Can you bring her over to identify the body? After that, I will interview you."

Tessa left them and returned with her hand around Eloise's shoulders. "I've explained what you want her to do," Tessa said in a pragmatic tone.

"Mama Rose, would you mind?" The commissioner indicated towards the tablecloth.

Rose bent down and pulled back the cover.

Eloise's handsome face crumbled but she managed to mutter, "Yes, that's my sister. Becky, Rebecca Munro."

She turned and staggered back to her seat. Tessa rushed to assist her.

Commissioner Akida said in a monotone voice, "At least that's done." He looked around the restaurant. "I see Constable Wachira is still collecting witness details. So I need someone to remain with the body."

"I can do that," suggested Sam.

"And I'll stay with you," said Thabiti.

"Good. And I also need a volunteer to be a scribe until the constable can join us."

"Oh, can I?" asked Chloe. Her eyes shone.

Tessa rejoined them.

"Certainly, but you'll need a pen and paper," the commissioner told Chloe.

Tessa removed some paper from her clipboard. "You can use this, but I seem to have lost my pen."

As Chloe searched for a biro Pearl said, "If you don't need me I'll head home."

Commissioner Akida, Rose and Tessa entered the cool interior of the studio. A full-length mirror covered the back wall and a metre-high rail ran along in front of it. Beside the door was a rack of dumb-bells and a pile of light-blue yoga mats.

Commissioner Akida sat facing Tessa. Chloe bustled in and sat next to him, her newly acquired pen poised for action. Rose sat to one side so she could observe the proceedings.

Commissioner Akida began, "For the record, please can you confirm your name, address and contact number."

Tessa Newton provided her details and Rose noted that she lived in Hardy, in Nairobi. It was a less exclusive, and less expensive, suburb, than its neighbour Karen, which was a historically European area of the capital.

Rose asked, "We don't actually know much about the dead woman except her name. What can you tell us?"

"Becky was born in Kenya, but she was at school in England when her parents disappeared and she remained there. Somewhere in the south, I think. And she's engaged to an Englishman."

Up to this point Tessa had been matter-of-fact, as if she was dealing with a member of her tour group, but now she broke eye contact with Rose and looked down at the table, as she tugged on a strand of dark hair.

"I think she was only twenty-four or twenty-five and, despite her parent's tragedy, she still had a simple, trusting way of looking at life."

"Do you know why she was in Nanyuki?" asked the commissioner.

"I don't, you'll have to ask Eloise."

"We will. Where were you when she collapsed?"

"I guess I was sort of opposite her, next to Alex, my brother. We were all entranced by my niece, Mia, who was dancing in the middle of our group."

"And what did you see?"

"Nothing. As I said, my attention was drawn to Mia and I didn't even notice Becky fall to the floor. I only knew something was wrong when Eloise screamed."

"Thank you. You can leave with your tour group, but we may need to speak to you again."

Tessa looked down at her hands. "I wish I could be of more help. I'm around in Nanyuki for the next week or so organising a new group of travellers for a trip to Samburu."

Tessa stood and as she reached the door, Rose asked, "Can you ask Eloise to join us?"

CHAPTER FIFTEEN

E loise stepped into the studio followed by Guy.

"Please sit down." Commissioner Akida instructed, but with a note of sympathy in his voice.

As Eloise sat, Guy searched the room, presumably looking for another chair.

Commissioner Akida looked up at him and said, "Please can you leave us. You will have a chance to say what you need to in due course."

"But my wife needs me." Guy indicated towards Eloise.

"Don't worry, we understand that this is a very difficult time for you both," the commissioner said in a softer tone, "And it's not as if we are accusing either of you of anything." He looked across at Eloise. "We just need some information about your sister, so we can confirm the cause of death and put an end to this sad matter."

Eloise turned and placed a hand on her husband's leg. "I'll be OK. You go and sit with Alex and Hellen."

Guy left the room and the commissioner stated, "Please can you tell us your full name."

"Eloise Emma Ramsey."

Chloe wrote on a sheet of paper.

"And your sister's name and date of birth."

"Rebecca Catherine Munro. 17th February 1991."

Eloise continued to answer the commissioner's questions, giving her address in Karen, Nairobi, and her date of birth, which made her twenty-nine years old. She confirmed that Becky lived in Gloucestershire in England, and that she was engaged to be married.

Eloise's hand flew to her mouth. "What about her fiancé, Edward? He needs to be told what has happened."

"How well do you know him?" asked Rose.

"I don't. I met him last summer when I visited Becky in the UK, but that's all."

"If you can provide his contact details, I will ask one of my officers to contact him," proposed the commissioner.

"Yes, thank you. I have his number in my phone." She looked around, "Which I must have left in my bag."

"We'll sort that out later. I think Mama Rose has some questions about your sister's medical history."

Rose cleared her throat. "The doctor believes she died from a heart attack ..."

"Heart attack. But she's too young," cried Eloise.

"So she hadn't been diagnosed with a heart condition, or suffered any previous attacks?" probed Rose.

"No!" Eloise was indignant. "She was as fit as a cheetah and completed the Lewa Half Marathon last month."

Rose continued calmly. "Did she have any other medical conditions? Had she been ill recently or suffered from any inflammatory diseases?"

"No. No. No." A sheen of sweat appeared on Eloise's forehead.

Rose held her hands up in a conciliatory gesture. "I'm sorry I have to ask these questions, but it's like the commissioner said, until we establish the cause of death, the case will remain open, and your sister's body won't be released."

Eloise placed both hands on the table and took a deep breath. "I'm sorry. What else do you want to know? She didn't have any medical conditions that I was aware of, and she didn't tell me she had been ill recently."

Rose changed tack slightly and hoped the commissioner didn't mind her diverging from the medical questions. She asked, "I understand your parents disappeared. Do you mind telling us what happened, and if you think it adversely affected your sister in terms of stress, or drove her to use drugs or abuse alcohol?"

Eloise bristled again. "My sister did not take drugs and yes, she did drink, but no more than the rest of us." She looked over the commissioner's shoulder at the mirrored wall and quickly down at the table.

"My parents, Michael and Geraldine Munro," she spoke mechanically, "disappeared in 2007. My father was flying them home from Nairobi. Wilson Airport lost contact just before the Aberdare Mountain range, and although their plane has never been found, it is presumed they crashed and died."

There was silence in the room.

"I returned to Kenya, but Becky stayed at school in England. She never really came to terms with the fact that they were dead."

"Did this have anything to do with your sister's current visit?" the commissioner asked shrewdly.

"Yes. My parents have been missing for nearly nine years, but the Kenyan courts require certain criteria to be met before they determine that a missing person can be declared legally dead. This is at the discretion of the court, which has not been very keen on accepting my parents' death. I suspect it has something to do with the life assurance company which is opposing the petition."

"And did this worry your sister?" asked Rose.

"It bothered us both. To lose your parents is one thing, but not to be able to grieve for them is another. We haven't even been able to hold a memorial service."

"But you don't think this caused your sister's death?" pressed Rose.

"Why would it? Sure, we've spent some long days in lawyers' offices in Nairobi, and in court which is not a pleasant experience, but my parents disappeared a long time ago."

Rose tapped her fingers on her thigh and then asked, "What did Becky eat and drink today?"

"Why, what does that matter?"

"As I said, we are just looking at all possible angles," Rose reassured Eloise.

"She had a light breakfast. Some muesli and fruit. And before we arrived here she'd only drunk coffee and water. She'd perhaps had half a glass of white wine before she collapsed."

Rose turned to Commissioner Akida and said, "I'm afraid Eloise hasn't told us about anything which could have contributed to her sister's heart attack and death."

"The new coroner's not going to like this." The commissioner rolled his eyes. "She's bound to demand a postmortem."

"Poor Becky. Do they really have to cut her up?"

Rose noticed tears at the corner of Eloise's eyes and suggested, "How about starting with a blood test? And I believe the Cottage Hospital can now perform a post-mortem biopsy. People were objecting to full-blown autopsies on religious grounds."

The commissioner nodded and replied, "I can suggest that."

Eloise sniffed and wiped her eyes with her sleeve. "I'm sorry. This is all a bit much. Do what you have to. I want to find out why she died. It's just the thought of harming her I can't bear."

Eloise turned her head and a loud sob escaped. "Sorry," she repeated in a choked voice.

The commissioner cleared his throat and looked at Rose.

Rose stood and moved across to the stricken woman, and placed a hand on her shoulder.

"There's no need to apologise. I recently lost my husband, so I do understand. The first step in the grieving process is to accept your sister's death. It's very hard to do without knowing the how and the why." She helped Eloise to her feet.

"Why don't you return to your friends and we'll arrange for your sister's body to be collected."

CHAPTER SIXTEEN

C onstable Wachira entered the studio as Eloise left.

"I think I've collected the names and addresses of all the witnesses, sir, although there were a lot of them."

"Thank you, Constable. I hope this will be a straightforward matter and we won't need to interview them all."

"Sam has asked me if there is any decision about the body." She lowered her voice, "It's very warm outside and ... well, it's not ideal."

"Enough said. Please, can you contact the mortuary at the Cottage Hospital and ask them to collect the body. Tell them Dr Farrukh believes the deceased died as a result of a heart attack, but that we've been unable to establish the exact cause of death. The next of kin would prefer not to have a full autopsy, so Mama Rose suggested we start with an analysis of her blood, and a biopsy of her heart. Have you got that all down?"

"Biopsy of the heart," repeated the young constable as she wrote in her notebook. "Yes sir, I'll call them right away."

"Before you do, can you ask the sister's husband to join us," requested the commissioner.

"Which is he?"

"Tall, fair hair…"

"Oh, the attractive one."

"Is he?" queried the commissioner.

"I think so, don't you, Chloe?" enquired Constable Wachira.

Chloe had remained silent during Eloise's interview, but she now grinned, "Absolutely."

The commissioner leaned back and looked warily at the women. "Yes, well, can you ask him to join us?"

Constable Wachira had just reached the doorway when Alex Newton walked in holding hands with the girl in the pink dress. He was followed by Hellen who was carrying her toddler on her hip.

"I'm sorry to interrupt, but can my wife take the children home? It's very hot for them and Mia is ... rather upset," Alex mouthed the last words and the girl looked up at him as she sucked her thumb.

"Do you live in Nanyuki?" the commissioner asked.

"Yes, we recently moved into a new house on the Muthaiga estate," replied Alex.

Hellen stared at the floor as she adjusted the toddler's position on her hip.

"I think we can let them go, Commissioner. I'm not sure Hellen will be able to add anything to the statements we already have, and we're also interviewing the dead woman's brother-in-law," remarked Rose.

"I'm going to stay with Guy anyway," stated Alex, "and be with Eloise when you interview him."

Hellen looked up with watery eyes, and pleaded, "Can't you come home with us?"

Alex cleared his throat. "Come now, it's not far and if you don't want to drive, it won't take you long to walk." He ushered his family out of the room.

Thabiti popped his head round the door. "Is it OK if I leave now?"

"Yes, of course Thabiti," confirmed the commissioner. "I'll let you know if I need to speak with you."

Thabiti turned, and stepped quickly back as the elegant figure of Guy Ramsey entered the studio. Guy sat down without being offered a seat and crossed his legs.

"How can I help?" he asked lazily as he removed a pair of aviator sunglasses.

Thabiti waved and left.

"I just want to get things straight in my mind," the commissioner said. "You are Guy Ramsey, husband of Eloise, and the dead woman was your sister-in-law."

"That's correct," Guy said, his voice flat.

"Can you tell us what you saw, and what you think happened to your sister-in-law."

"Sure, I was talking with Fergus ..."

"Who's Fergus?"

"A lawyer from Nairobi, Fergus Peacock."

The commissioner leaned forward and checked Chloe's notes. He sat up and said, "Please continue."

"As I was saying, my attention was drawn to Mia, Hellen and Alex's daughter, who was spinning round and round and laughing. The next minute Eloise screamed and Becky was lying on the floor. And that's it."

"Did you see anything strange or unusual?"

"This is Kenya, so there's always something. I did see Otto walk past. He's a childhood friend of Becky's, but I understand he's been bothering her recently."

Rose pinched her nose. She was uncertain if Guy was being helpful or deliberately implicating Otto in something, as yet undiscovered.

"Do you know where I can find this Otto?" asked the commissioner.

"He's usually hanging around Dormans or up at the North Kenya Polo Club."

"Thank you. Finally, can you tell me where everyone was when Rebecca Munro collapsed?"

Guy crossed his arms. "I was standing next to Fergus on Becky's right-hand side, and Eloise was standing to her left. In front of her was the dancing Mia. I think Alex and that sister of his, Tessa, were on the far side. And Hellen was sitting at the table with young Liam."

After Guy had left, the commissioner stood and paced the length of the small studio.

He turned and remarked, "Everything points to death from natural causes. I know she was young and fit, but it's not unheard of for such people to collapse and die. Particularly if she had been suffering from stress or depression following her parents' disappearance. Her sister might not have known about it. Equally, nobody can confirm or deny that she took drugs in England or drank excessively."

"I don't think she did," interjected Rose. "Although it's just my impression from the little I saw of her and the way the witnesses spoke about her."

The commissioner started pacing again. "Hopefully, once the autopsy has been completed we can wrap this case up."

He stopped by the table and enquired, "Mama Rose, don't you agree?"

She leaned back. "It certainly looks that way but ... I just have an ominous feeling. It's the same sense of foreboding which kept drawing me back to the group earlier. There was nothing I could put my finger on, just the impression of dark undertones."

Chloe turned to Rose and laid a hand on her knee. "Are you sure you weren't just feeling troubled because it was the first time you have been out since ... for a while?"

Rose placed her hand over Chloe's. "I'm sure you're right."

The commissioner secured his cap on his head.

"I had better report the death to our new coroner. It is one of her first cases, so I do hope she doesn't complicate it."

CHAPTER SEVENTEEN

On Tuesday morning, Rose walked into the Dormans complex and found Chloe seated at the table to the right-hand side of the entrance.

Chloe stood and greeted Rose. "Thanks for coming. There's something I wanted to discuss with you. But first, do you have any news of Becky Munro's death?"

Rose sat down and shook her head. "I've not heard anything. I guess the police believe she died of natural causes, so that's probably the end of the matter."

"Don't you believe it," announced Thabiti as he slipped onto an empty seat. He unfolded a newspaper and handed it to Rose. She didn't have her glasses, so she squinted at a photograph of the Bushman's Restaurant, and another of a very large African woman standing in front of Nanyuki's County Court building.

Thabiti pointed at the photograph, "That's our new coroner, Fatima Rotich."

"I didn't know we had an old coroner," commented Chloe, as she swivelled the paper round and examined the photograph. "Commissioner Akida's standing behind her and he doesn't look very happy."

Thabiti leaned forward. "I'm not surprised. Ms Rotich announced that there will be an inquest into Rebecca Munro's death, and that the police will be interviewing all the witnesses." He sat up. "So that includes us. Poor Constable Wachira is going to be busy, but at least it'll keep her away from traffic duty."

Rose clenched her hands. "But she's supposed to be studying for her sergeant's exams."

"Well, maybe this will be good practice for her," suggested Chloe.

Rose turned to her. "Perhaps. Anyway, why did you want to meet me?"

"Oh, yes. I had a call from Dan last night. Can you believe it? I've entered his team for The Great Grevy's Rally, and now they can't make it. Some important dignitary is visiting the site and they all have to remain on duty. Anyway, he's asked me to take a team in their place."

"What is The Great Grevy's Rally?" asked Thabiti.

"It's a conservation initiative to count the number of surviving Grevy's zebra through an on-the-ground census," replied Rose.

Chloe explained, "According to the email Dan forwarded to me, Grevy's zebra are rarer than black rhino, and their numbers have dropped from fifteen thousand, in the nineteen seventies, to just two thousand today."

"And I think most of those are in northern Kenya, with a few in southern Ethiopia," added Rose.

"That's right," agreed Chloe. "The event is this weekend. Would you like to join me? Our census area is in Samburu National Reserve, a hundred and thirty kilometres north of here. And we don't need to worry about rooms and food as they are already covered by Dan's company."

"I'm not sure I want to be away all weekend," confided Rose.

Chloe looked across at Thabiti. "You'll come, won't you?"

He pulled at the corner of the newspaper. "When are you leaving?"

Chloe's eyes glowed. "On Friday afternoon. We'll have supper at the lodge so we're ready for the early start on Saturday morning."

Thabiti rubbed his nose. "I'm afraid I can't. I'm going on a plane hunting expedition on Friday."

Chloe's eyes narrowed.

"Pete Stephenson is leading a search for wreckage to identify a World War II bomber which crashed on the Aberdare Range. And he's asked me to film their progress."

Chloe had a pinched expression as she said, "It's really annoying Dan can't take part." She leaned back, "But I suppose he can't help it. And the event is important for wildlife conservation, so I don't want to let the organisers down."

Rose thought back to Gabriel Baker proudly taking entries. He had looked far more confident and mature than when Rose first met him at the Laikipia Conservation Society Conference in April. Then he had epitomised a student with long, dank hair, tied back in a ponytail.

Chloe looked so vulnerable as she wet her lips, and she was right, the event was all about wildlife conservation, and was extremely important. Conservationists needed information, not only about the number of Grevy's zebra, but also their age, sex and location, if they were to find a way to support the species and increase their numbers.

Her mind was drawn to earlier, happier days, sitting on the banks of the Ewaso Nyiro River, which separated Samburu National Reserve from the neighbouring Buffalo Springs Reserve to the south.

She and Craig had enjoyed a picnic as they watched elephants cross the river and herds of impala approach in a skittish manner as they sought water. Although only two hours' drive from Nanyuki, the reserves were much drier and the heat more intense than in Laikipia.

Craig had enjoyed the opportunity to see not only Grevy's zebra, but also the rare Beisa oryx, Somali ostriches and an abundance of bird life. He would want her to go and support the Grevy's Zebra Trust, and it might be beneficial to get away from Nanyuki for the weekend, especially if she didn't have to pay for the trip.

Rose leaned towards Chloe, who was twisting her wedding band. "I'll come. And you're right. We need to do our bit to preserve the endangered Grevy's zebra."

Thabiti looked up, "And why don't you ask Pearl?"

"That's a great idea," beamed Chloe. "Now I've no idea where the waiters are today. I'll go inside and order. Tea, Rose?"

Rose nodded.

"Thabiti?"

Thabiti stood. "No thanks. I've things to do." He turned back to Rose. "I've ordered your air conditioning filter, but I'm waiting for it to arrive at Mr Obado's garage. Once it has, I'll pop round and fit it."

As he reached the entrance, he stepped back as Guy Ramsey strode through, followed by Alex Newton. They sat down at their usual corner table, next to Rose.

Alex leaned forward and asked, "So when are you going to meet our friend in Samburu?"

"I thought I might head up tomorrow," replied Guy.

"Do you have the twenty thousand shillings he demanded?"

"No, but I'll get it. Or I might buy him a sheep and see if he'll settle for ten thousand."

Chloe returned as Hellen Newton joined Alex and Guy, and asked, "How's Eloise?"

"She's consoling herself by shopping." Guy's lips pressed together.

Chloe picked up her mobile phone.

"In Nanyuki?" questioned Hellen. "I've no idea what would interest her here. I have to travel to Nairobi for everything except food."

"Even the wine selection is limited," muttered Alex.

"Eloise heard about the opening of a new homeware shop which she wanted to check out," remarked Guy.

Rose felt a movement behind her and looked around as Eloise Ramsey stepped through the iron archway into the courtyard.

She wore dark glasses and her hair was tied up in a loose bun at the back of her head. Wispy strands escaped and she brushed them away as she looked around. Spotting Alex, Guy and Hellen, she wandered over to join them and sat down, placing a large carrier bag by her feet.

"Did you find anything nice?" Hellen asked warmly.

"There were a few interesting pieces."

Guy and Alex returned to their conversation.

Eloise removed a wooden box, inlaid with ivory and the size of a small pencil case, from her bag and handed it to Hellen. "Can you look after this for me, and if I don't get a chance to ask for it back, please open it." Eloise looked across at Guy and Alex and back to Hellen. "And promise me you won't show it to anyone."

Hellen looked perplexed but nodded her assent.

Chloe interrupted Rose's musings and said, "I've sent Pearl a message asking if she'd like to join us this weekend."

Rose was distracted again as Eloise pulled a large cushion out of the carrier bag. It was embroidered with an African scene and a zebra. "I thought this would look nice on the veranda. Add some colour."

Rose also liked the cushion and thought she had seen it, or something similar, before.

At last, Rose's tea and Chloe's cappuccino arrived. Rose concentrated on preparing her tea, so she was surprised when she heard a young man's raised voice at the table beside her. She glanced up and saw the fair-haired Otto standing in front of Eloise.

"I told you to persuade Becky to stay, and now look what's happened. It's all your fault," Otto cried in an accusatory tone.

Eloise blinked rapidly.

"Otto, that's enough. You were the one pestering Becky," said Guy harshly. He looked across at Hellen and then back to Otto. "And you threatened her."

"Guy, that's not what happened," implored Hellen.

"I think it is. And now he's feeling guilty and trying to blame Eloise. As if she isn't upset enough," Guy said, glaring at Hellen.

"I'm not blaming Eloise. Not directly. But she shouldn't have let Becky consider selling Roho House. Especially if it's to the new brewery. You know what happened last time." Otto stared at Hellen and raised his eyebrows. "Some things are best left undisturbed, aren't they?"

CHAPTER EIGHTEEN

That afternoon, Rose leaned back against the striped cushions of her large, cedar sofa on her outdoor patio. Kipto had scattered crumbs and scraps from the kitchen on the stone bird table which stood at the edge of the garden, underneath the bottlebrush tree.

She watched the iridescent blue and green backs of superb starlings as they landed on the bird table to claim their edible prizes. Amongst them was a blue-black coloured bird, with a white belly and yellow eyes.

It was too small to be a magpie, and was similar in size and shape to the surrounding starlings. Craig would have known what species it was, but he would still have consulted his bird book.

Rose peeled herself off the sofa, wandered into the living room and searched the bookcase for the white bound *Birds of East Africa* book. It lay on its side, at the front of the second shelf, where it must have been left the final time Craig used it.

Returning outside, she searched for superb starlings in the index and turned to a well-thumbed page. Flicking back several pages, she came across the image of a two species of black and white starling.

The one with yellow eyes was an Abbott's starling. She read that it was rare to see because the number of birds had dwindled as their native forest habitat was lost. One of the locations they could still be found was Mount Kenya.

Rose watched the little black and white bird, visiting from its forest home, and her chest ached. How many more creatures were battling against extinction because of the action of men? People who wanted more land, and more wealth.

Kipto knocked on the open patio door.

Rose looked up at her with watery eyes.

"You not sleep then," Kipto said ruefully. "Policewoman here to see you."

Constable Wachira stepped out onto the patio. "Sorry, I thought you might be in your shamba, but Kipto saw me and told me you were on the patio."

Kipto still hovered in the doorway.

"Would you like some tea?" Rose offered the young constable.

"Yes, please," she replied in a grateful tone. "My mouth feels as dry as a lizard's after asking so many questions today."

She wore her police uniform, which consisted of a navy skirt and a white short-sleeved shirt. "May I sit at your table?" She asked.

"Of course." Rose stood up, and as she joined the young policewoman, she enquired, "I presume this isn't a social call."

The constable placed her notebook and pen on the table and explained, "Commissioner Akida had a heated exchange with the new coroner, Ms Rotich, this morning. The previous coroner rarely interfered with police business, but Ms Rotich appears keen to make her mark. She's ordered the police to gather information for her about Rebecca Munro's death."

"Which means?" enquired Rose.

"That I have to interview every witness, although the commissioner said that when people start repeating what others have told me, and don't provide any new information, I can stop. So I thought I'd begin with those who were closest to the deceased when she collapsed. Which includes you. I hope you don't mind."

Kipto returned with the tea things, which included a teapot and a plate of homemade biscuits.

"You're honoured," announced Rose. "I didn't know we still had that tea pot. And biscuits, that's a rarity."

Constable Wachira poured them both cups of tea and asked, "What can you tell me about yesterday's incident?" She picked up a biscuit.

Rose nursed her cup and thought. Out loud she began, "There was something about the group Rebecca Munro was with, which kept drawing my attention. But I can't put my finger on what it was. There were certainly tensions. Alex Newton and his sister, the tour guide, immediately come to mind. I overheard them discussing work, their father's business, and money, or lack of it."

Constable Wachira consulted her notes. She read, "Mr Newton senior set up Horizon Safaris in the 1980s, specialising in bespoke safari packages for small groups. He died in 2010 and left the business to his son, Alex."

She looked up. "Sam thinks he remembers an incident where the sister 'kidnapped' a tour group after she and her brother had a row about the business at a lodge. She left the company and has been guiding in Kenya, Tanzania and Ethiopia. I believe Sam respects her, which is more than can be said for Guy Ramsey, Alex's business partner. Sam said he's a work-shy playboy who lives beyond his means."

Rose laughed at Sam's description of Guy but couldn't help feeling sorry for Eloise.

Constable Wachira consulted her notes once again. "Guy Ramsey became a partner in Horizon Safaris in 2012, a year after he had married Eloise Munro. It seems to be common knowledge that he used her money to buy into the business."

"And did Sam tell you anything about the company? Is it in financial trouble?"

"He's not sure. But he heard a rumour that Alex Newton owes the Wambugu family in Nairobi money. He thinks it's one reason the Newtons relocated to Nanyuki."

"Other people's lives are always far more fascinating than our own," Rose mused.

"Is there anything else you can tell me?" asked Constable Wachira.

"That snake of a lawyer, Fergus Peacock, was upsetting Hellen Munro. Have you spoken to her?"

"No, I haven't had a chance. She's always out on appointments whenever I drop by the office, or at least that's what the notice on her office door states. I thought I would call again when I'm finished here."

"When you do speak to her, I think it would be worthwhile asking why she was writing Fergus Peacock a cheque. Although it may turn out to be nothing to do with this business, but ..." Rose's gaze fell once more on the birds on the bird table.

The constable jotted something in her notebook before she looked up and asked, "Did you actually see Rebecca Munro collapse?"

Rose squeezed her eyes shut and replied, "No. Sorry. I was watching the girl in the pink dress."

Constable Wachira sat back. "I think most people were. She certainly distracted me as I followed a young man out of the toilet block."

Rose scratched her cheek. "The girl in the pink dress. Is she Hellen and Alex Newton's daughter?"

Constable Wachira picked up her notebook and flicked through several pages. "She is called Mia. She's six years old and attends Podo School in Nanyuki. Her brother is Liam, aged two. Hellen was sitting at the end of the table, feeding him, when Rebecca collapsed."

The young constable ploughed on with her questions. "When you were attending to Rebecca, did you notice anything unusual?"

Rose sipped her tea. "It was obvious to all that she was having a fit by the way she convulsed and threw her limbs around. I remember Guy Ramsey commenting that her lips were blue, which I knew meant she was having trouble breathing. She opened her eyes just once when she spoke and said, 'Please help me'. Then her pulse slowed as she slipped into unconsciousness and her heart stopped."

A mobile phone rang. "Excuse me," said Constable Wachira as she answered it, but she remained seated at the table. "Another one?" She listened and then responded, "Yes, I'll go straight over."

The call ended and Constable Wachira placed both her arms on the table and slumped forward.

Rose noticed dark bags underneath the constable's eyes. She asked, "What's happened?"

"Another break in," replied the young constable. "I told you someone burgled Mrs Sharpe's house on Sunday morning. It appears they've struck again."

CHAPTER NINETEEN

Rose woke late on Wednesday morning. Groggily she tried to hold on to the fading memory of her dream and as it disappeared she felt a sense of loss. And a yearning for her childhood, so long ago.

Sleepily she reached across to Craig's side of the bed but, instead of his warm body, her hand touched fur. She tried to flex her stiff arthritic fingers as she stroked Izzy, who purred contentedly.

Rose rolled onto her back and stared at the mottled ceiling. Gradually the sounds of Nanyuki permeated the walls of her cottage: the sharp beep of a horn, the cry of a young child and the low moo of Bette, her cow.

Did she need to get up today? She could ride Whoosh, or write an overdue email to Heather, or sort through a box file of Craig's photographs she'd recently found in his office.

She also needed to decide on a suitable trophy to be presented in Craig's memory at the following month's Mugs Mug Polo competition. She smiled, remembering that Dickie Chambers had also commissioned a portrait of Craig for the clubhouse.

It was good to know other people were still thinking of Craig and that he wasn't a forgotten memory. And he would have been so chuffed to know that his portrait was to hang on the clubhouse wall, where it could look down on the younger players, worse for wear from an evening of celebration, or share a toast with the older members.

Rose felt a draft, and heard a patter of paws on the concrete floor. Potto jumped onto her bed and attempted to lick her face.

"No, you don't." She grabbed Potto and placed her on top of the ruffled duvet.

"Chamgei," called Kipto as she tapped on the partially open door and entered. "Good. You sleep long," she said in a satisfied tone. She placed a cup of tea beside Rose's bed.

As Rose sat up she heard her phone ring.

Kipto, with her hands on her hips, commented, "There it go again. It keep making buzz buzz noise. Don't people know you allowed to rest?"

Rose smiled indulgently. "Can you fetch it for me? Dr Emma might need my help with a patient."

Kipto returned with the phone, but the ringing had stopped. Rose reached for her glasses on the bedside table and squinted at the small screen. She clicked to missed calls and was surprised to find Commissioner Akida's number. She pressed it.

The commissioner answered, "Habari, Mama Rose. Sorry to keep calling. I guess you were busy with a patient."

"Something like that." Rose flinched at the small lie.

"I'm meeting Dr Farrukh at the mortuary department of the Cottage Hospital at ten o'clock. Would you like to join us?"

Rose glanced at her watch. It was nine thirty. She had slept in. "Yes, I'll be there," she confirmed.

Rose dressed quickly, brushed her hair and teeth and washed her face. Outside, she found the forlorn sight of the breakfast table set for one. She missed not starting the day with Craig. As she sat down, she felt as if someone was squeezing her heart.

She smelt warm toast and looked up gratefully as Kipto brought her two slices for her breakfast.

Twenty minutes later, Rose joined Commissioner Akida and Dr Farrukh outside the single-storey mortuary building, at the rear of the Cottage Hospital.

"And some disinfectant," the pathologist instructed a wiry looking man. The wiry man eyed the newcomers with suspicion, picked up his mobile phone and left the mortuary.

The pathologist reached for a fresh pair of latex gloves, from a box on his desk, and instructed, "Come this way, but I don't have much to tell you."

He lifted the cloth covering the naked form of Rebecca Munro. Rose and the commissioner stood back and allowed Dr Farrukh to examine the body.

"As you can see," explained the pathologist, "the only marks on her are a scar from knee surgery, which I would estimate is four or five years old, a scratch on her left leg, and a small wound on her upper right arm.

The pathologist replaced the cloth and said, "We didn't perform a full autopsy, but I took tissue samples of her heart. I'm afraid that as far as I can tell it was perfectly healthy."

"Did the lab find anything significant when they analysed her blood?" asked Dr Farrukh.

"No, they didn't. Although that doesn't mean there wasn't a poisonous substance. Do you know what poison we should be looking for? We kept several blood samples in case we need to test for something specific in the future."

"I'm sorry. I'm rather clutching at straws," confessed Dr Farrukh. "There's no reason to think she ate or drank anything that caused her death."

"Is that so?" demanded a voice which made Rose jump.

"Stay behind me," hissed the commissioner.

A large African woman filled the doorway. She wore a bright red and yellow traditionally patterned dress which hung shapelessly on her huge figure. Most of her hair appeared to be brushed forward over the left side of her face, and it contained red and yellow streaks. She glared at them through thick, black-rimmed glasses.

"Why wasn't I informed about this meeting, Commissioner?" Her voice was deep and Rose suspected her volume switch was permanently stuck on loud.

"Good morning, Ms Rotich. Let me introduce Dr Farrukh, who has been discussing the pathologist's findings. At this stage I am purely an observer."

"So what can you tell me, Doctor?" Ms Rotich demanded.

"Nothing," declared the doctor. She turned to the pathologist and said, "Thank you."

"Nothing," repeated the newcomer.

"Yes, that's right. We have not been able to establish why Rebecca Munro died. Now if you don't mind, I have patients to attended to." She squeezed past the large woman who stepped towards the commissioner.

"I expect to be kept informed of all and every meeting in respect of this case. I am the coroner."

Rose peered around the commissioner, hoping to get a better view of the woman.

"And who are you?" Ms Rotich demanded.

"Um." Rose replied weakly.

Dr Farrukh called from the doorway. "Come along, Rose. We have people to see."

Rose exhaled and despite her wobbly legs she squeezed past the overweight woman who now faced the Commissioner.

The Commissioner's phone rang and Rose heard him stifle a laugh. He said, "Excuse me. I need to take this call."

Dr Farrukh, Rose and the commissioner rushed out of the mortuary and dissolved into laughter. Behind them they could hear Ms Rotich interrogating the pathologist.

The wiry man they had encountered earlier leaned against a wall, grinning.

"At least we know how she found out about the meeting," observed Rose, indicating towards the wiry man.

"You're going to have to be careful, Commissioner. That woman will soon have spies everywhere," added Dr Farrukh.

"Anyway, that was a lucky escape Commissioner. Who called you?" asked Rose.

He grinned and looked across at Dr Farrukh in a conspiratorial manner.

"You did?" cried Rose. "Quick thinking."

"I couldn't leave him in there unprotected from that woman. Come on. Let's retire to my office, out of the way of prying eyes and ears."

CHAPTER TWENTY

D r Farrukh sat behind her desk and placed the tips of her fingers together.

She said, "Technically Ms Rotich is right. I can only certify that Rebecca Munro died of a heart attack, but not the reason for it. Without confirmation that her death is from natural causes, the coroner is perfectly within her rights, in fact some would say it is her duty, to continue the investigation. And in due course hold an inquest."

Rose mused, "There's no indication she committed suicide or was killed by an unknown party. And there's nothing to show there was an accident of any kind. She may have hit her head when she fell, but the pathologist didn't highlight any damage to her skull."

"Correct," agreed Dr Farrukh. "And without further evidence there is nothing more I can do."

The commissioner stood and paced the room. "I have a feeling Ms Rotich is going to milk the occasion to highlight perceived police incompetence, and establish her role as coroner and overseer of justice."

Rose nodded, "And if she gets her elbows out, I'm afraid you'll be on the losing side, Commissioner."

"Agreed, so I, the police, need to proceed with caution, care and diligence. Which is why I need to keep Constable Wachira on the case, even though she should be studying for her sergeants' exams."

Dr Farrukh stated with finality, "My job's done unless you find new evidence."

Rose murmured, "It's the family I feel sorry for. Until the coroner releases her body, they can't bury or cremate her."

"That may be true, but I think we're done here," said the commissioner. "Thank you both for your assistance."

Rose pushed back her chair and asked, "Is Mrs Sharpe still here?"

"Yes, she's in D ward," replied Dr Farrukh.

"I promised Constable Wachira I would visit her, following her break in, and it's very remiss of me, but I haven't done so yet."

Commissioner Akida and Rose left Dr Farrukh's office and turned, walking away in opposite directions.

Rose pushed open the door of one of the Cottage Hospital's larger wards. Eight of the ten beds were occupied and light and air spilled in from the open patio doors at the far end.

Winnie Sharpe was propped up in a sitting position on her bed reading a book. Rose found a plastic chair and carried it across.

"Rose, how wonderful to see you. I get so few visitors," smiled the older woman.

Rose felt guilty that she had not brought a present or any flowers. Winnie's thin white arms extended out of a short-sleeved cotton night dress. She still tied her grey hair in a bun on top of her head, but it was thin and her pink scalp was clearly visible.

"I'm sorry, I haven't brought you anything," apologised Rose.

"I don't need things, it's company I yearn for these days. I've been very lonely since Arthur passed away. And how are you? I heard about your husband's passing."

"Yes, Craig died a few weeks ago. It's probably a blessing as he was in a lot of pain from a secondary complication to polio which he contracted as a child."

"Of course, I remember he walked with a limp. So we can keep each other company." Winnie smiled warmly.

She looked at Rose over the top of her half-moon glasses and Rose could envisage her in her former days as a schoolteacher.

Winnie declared, "I want to go home." Then she dropped her voice and whispered, "I can't afford to stay here, but my house has been burgled so the doctor won't let me leave."

"I'm sorry to hear about your break in."

Winnie waved the comment away with the flick of her hand. "What have I got left to steal? Anything of value is here with me in hospital. After eighty-one years, my most treasured possessions fit into a single bag. But that's not what matters, is it?"

"No," agreed Rose. "It's not." But she thought of her small cottage with its abundance of flowers in the front garden, the chickens pecking the ground in front of the stables, and Bette the cow, grazing peacefully with Bahati and Whoosh.

Rose entered her cottage through the rear kitchen door.

Kipto greeted her, "Chamgei, Mama. The landlord visit. I told him about leaky roof."

She pointed up at a stained section of plasterboard.

"Thank you. Do you know what he wanted?"

"He bring woman with him and they walk around house and point at things. I heard them in your bathroom. They say something about new shower."

A shower, thought Rose. That would be a great addition to the bathroom, which currently only had a scratched yellow bathtub. Perhaps the landlord was going to make some improvements. Then she felt a chill run down her spine. As long as he didn't increase her rent to pay for them.

CHAPTER TWENTY-ONE

Thabiti drove his motorbike along the bumpy track leading to Mama Rose's cottage and stopped outside her black metal gates. He sounded his horn and waited.

From the opposite direction, a white Probox approached and pulled to a stop beside him. Dr Emma was driving and beside her was Hellen Newton, the new estate agent.

He walked forward and asked through the open window, "Habari, are you also visiting Mama Rose?"

Dr Emma didn't respond but instead turned towards her passenger. "Hellen, I don't understand. Why have you brought me to Mama Rose's house?"

"Rose? As in the lady who works with you? And took me to the Women's League meeting?"

"Yes, that Rose. This is where she lives."

Hellen placed her hands on the dashboard, "But the owner showed me around the property yesterday. He's looking to sell it and told me the current occupant is leaving."

Thabiti heard a rattle and clang as the bolts were drawn back on the gate.

Kipto's head appeared. "You all come to see Mama? In, in," she indicated as she opened the gate wider.

Thabiti pushed his motorbike and Dr Emma parked at the side of the house, outside Craig's office door.

"Mama work in shamba. Come," instructed Kipto.

Dr Emma marched along beside Kipto, whilst Hellen hung back with Thabiti.

She said in a strained voice, "Hello, I'm Hellen. I've seen you with Rose, haven't I?"

Thabiti shoved his hands in his pockets and looked down at the ground. He felt the familiar tightening in his chest and wondered if he should return later to see Mama Rose.

Hellen stopped and peered at him. "Are you all right? Have I said something to upset you?"

"I'm fine," Thabiti stuttered. He stopped and looked at Hellen. "It's Mama Rose that isn't. She and her husband Craig, they've lived in this house since he retired. She looks after it really well, and provides a home for rescue animals. She'll be devastated if you throw her out. Craig only just died and she can't afford somewhere else in Nanyuki. Not with room for all her animals."

Thabiti stopped speaking, stepped back and took a deep breath, trying to alleviate the tightness in his chest.

Hellen reached forward but he flinched away from her touch. "I am sorry but I'm only following my client's instructions. She needs to speak to him, to her landlord."

Hellen turned and followed the path Dr Emma had taken around the back of the house.

Thabiti looked around him. It was an attractive property and the front reminded him of pictures of English country gardens. When he had joined Craig for their morning crossword puzzle sessions, he'd felt a calmness as he'd inhaled the mixed scent of flowers.

Craig had enjoyed watching the birds investigate the stone bird table or land at the far side of the garden. Thabiti had often collected the bird book from inside the house so Craig could check he knew the name of a particular bird. And he usually did.

Thabiti walked around the side of the house. The field, where Bette the cow grazed, was a reasonable size. Many similar sized areas in Nairobi now had housing estates built on them and he supposed this would too, in time.

He didn't know much about property, but he could understand that the low density of buildings, the size of the plot, and its proximity to central Nanyuki made it an interesting investment opportunity.

He found Dr Emma and Hellen standing beside Mama Rose, who was kneeling on the ground spreading green leaves over a blue tarpaulin. Samwell, who had looked after Craig so well when he was ill, tipped out another bucket of leaves. Kipto bent over at her waist, and used her hands to deftly spread the new batch around.

Hellen asked, "What are you doing?"

"Drying chamomile leaves so I can use them in my herbal animal mixes," replied Rose.

"Rose, we really need to talk," Dr Emma pleaded. "The leaves can wait. My news cannot."

Mama Rose looked up at Dr Emma's pained expression and her eyebrows drew together in concern. She reached up with an arm and Dr Emma pulled her to her feet.

"Let's go the house. I feel like a cup of tea, anyway." She brushed her hands on her trousers, turned to Kipto who was still bent over the tarpaulin and asked, "Chai, tafadali."

Thabiti settled himself into Craig's old cedar chair. Dr Emma took the matching chair, and Mama Rose sat on the large sofa and swung her legs. Hellen retreated to the cane chair at the far end of the patio.

They sat in an uncomfortable silence as Kipto handed out cups of tea. There were no biscuits.

"I finish herbs," Kipto announced and left them.

Dr Emma spoke first. "Hellen, I think you need to explain the situation to Mama Rose."

"What situation?" Mama Rose asked, pulling at her chin.

Hellen placed her cup on a small table beside her and said, "I visited this property yesterday with the landlord. His daughter is getting married so he wants to sell it and buy her somewhere to live in Nairobi. He led me to understand that the current occupant would be leaving soon, and instructed me to start marketing it straight away."

Before Mama Rose had time to answer, Dr Emma interjected, "But he can't throw Rose out." She turned to Mama Rose, "What does your lease say?"

Mama Rose was very still and her mouth had fallen open. There was a pause before she answered, "Um ... I've no idea. Craig dealt with it."

Thabiti stood and said, "Let me see if I can find it."

He was relieved to leave the tense atmosphere and walked around the side of the house to Craig's office. Inside he examined the top row of files which he had helped Craig sort through. The first was labelled staff, the second utilities and the third management.

He removed the management file and opened it. The lease was inside, but he felt his stomach clench as he read the front page. It expired at the end of July. That was less than two weeks away.

He felt a pain at the back of his throat. This was his fault. He should have checked the lease. He'd promised Craig he would look after Mama Rose, but he'd failed her.

He returned to the patio with the folder. The women looked up expectantly, and Dr Emma's hand flew to her mouth as she exclaimed, "Oh no. You have bad news. I can see it in your face."

Thabiti opened the file and handed it to her. She started reading the lease and gasped, "Your tenancy finishes at the end of this month."

Hellen asked in a small voice, "Is there a clause requiring the landlord to give notice?"

"I've no idea. You look." Dr Emma's face was pinched.

Thabiti took the file and handed it to Hellen. "I'm sorry," he stammered, "this is my fault. I should have checked."

Mama Rose looked up at him and said in a monotone voice, "It's not your fault. I should also have checked, but I didn't know I had to ..." Her words tailed off.

Potto padded out of the house and jumped onto Mama Rose's lap and tried to lick her face.

Thabiti turned and walked into the garden. He could hear Dr Emma impatiently tapping her foot.

Hellen looked up and said in an apologetic tone, "There's no requirement for the landlord to give you notice. However, if he intends to sell the property, he must give you first refusal."

Mama Rose peered across at Hellen and asked, "What does that mean?"

"That you can buy it."

Mama Rose leaned back and shook her head. "I can't afford to pay Craig's hospital bills, never mind buy this house, and all the land. What's the asking price?"

"Twelve million shilling," Hellen replied.

Dr Emma whistled.

Thabiti thought, that's over a hundred thousand dollars and just under two and a half million shillings per acre. With prices in Nairobi reaching over fifty million shillings an acre, this property might be seen as good value for money. Kenyan people rarely thought long term, but they did like to own land.

"Oh dear, what am I to do?" Mama Rose's face crumpled.

CHAPTER TWENTY-TWO

After lunch, Rose was sitting on the patio staring out into the garden when Kipto announced, "Lady who come earlier is back."

Hellen Newton walked round the corner and stopped. She asked hesitantly, "May I speak with you?"

"Yes, I suppose so. I know it's not your fault, but it's a real blow to lose my house. Are there any other suitable properties with a rent of less than fifty thousand shillings a month?"

Hellen shook her head. "Nothing with land, and the houses that are available are rather soulless, rectangular buildings with bare concrete walls and windows with reflective coatings. I'm not sure you would be happy in any of them, but I'll keep looking for you. What about something outside Nanyuki? It might be cheaper."

Rose's shoulders slumped. "I don't have an awful lot of choice, do I?" She drew her knees up and hugged them. "I'm sure I could find something suitable in time, but that's not something I have. I really don't see how I can move out of here in less than two weeks."

"That's the reason I've come to see you. May I?" She indicated towards Craig's old chair.

Rose nodded.

Hellen sat down heavily, closed her eyes and rubbed her forehead.

After a few moments of silence she looked up at Rose and said, "I've spoken to the landlord and we've agreed that even if I do find a purchaser quickly, the legal aspects of the sale will take at least a month, probably two or three. He's agreed that you can stay until the end of August, and possibly September, depending on what progress has been made with the sale. I hope that gives you some breathing space."

Rose released her legs and leaned back against the sofa closing her eyes. "That is a relief. Thank you," she murmured.

Hellen picked at a thread hanging from her shirt and said, "I do understand what it's like losing your home. Not personally, but it's happened to my grandfather several times. His father lost his tribal land, well the British claimed it and redistributed it to mzungu settlers.

"My grandfather thought he'd get the land back after Independence but instead he was offered a small plot at Mogotio, north of Nakuru. He couldn't grow much as it was so hot and arid, but he found work on a nearby sisal estate and lived comfortably.

"But in the 1992 elections he was thrown off his plot. He lost his job and was given a parcel of land in another dry area, between Nakuru and Gilgil. But that area of the Rift Valley suffered huge tensions in the 2007 elections, and he was displaced again. This time he was offered land east of Nyahururu."

Rose said in a gentle tone, "I know the area you mean. The corrugated metal houses have blue roofs and it's very barren and rather lifeless."

Hellen nodded. "Exactly, I couldn't expect my elderly grandfather to move there, could I? But now he's going to lose his home again, and it's all my fault."

Rose leaned forward and asked, "Why do you think that?"

"Instead of taking the land near Nyahururu, I found a reclaimed plot near Nyeri, where our family were from originally. I agreed with the local council to stagger the purchase cost over ten years. But I don't have the money for the final payments. Unless I can find funds for this year's instalment, the council will repossess his land."

Rose looked out into her garden and said, "But you have your real estate job. Doesn't that help?"

"In time, I hope so. But not for the impending payment. My base salary is low. You see, I'll only earn decent money through commission when I buy, sell or rent property. That's why I've been so keen to meet local people. It's the reason I wanted to join the Women's League, but I think it'll be too late to help my granddad."

Rose rubbed her neck. "Perhaps you'll find a purchaser for this place quickly and earn some commission." She felt a sinking feeling in her stomach. "But please let me have August to sort myself out."

She studied the birds landing on the stone bird table and thought of Craig. "I suppose that whilst this has been our home for several years, and a place of refuge for my animals, I'll still have my memories when I leave. They are what's important to me."

"Of course," Hellen responded reflectively, "and my family are important to me."

CHAPTER TWENTY-THREE

After Hellen's visit Rose roused herself and asked Kipto and Samwell to help her bag up the camomile leaves, which had dried in the sun.

She heard a motorbike and then the beep of a horn. "I'll open the gate," she said. "I think that's Thabiti."

She pulled back the long horizontal bolt and opened the black metal gate.

"Habari," called Thabiti as he picked up his helmet and wheeled his motorbike inside. From his rucksack he removed a rectangular plastic-wrapped package. "I forgot to change your Land

Rover's air conditioning filter earlier. At least now I don't have to work out how to mend your kitchen roof."

He looked down at the ground and kicked at a patch of bare earth. "I spoke to Pearl at lunchtime, and if you don't find a place to stay, you're welcome to use our guest cottage."

"But I thought your father was living there?" replied Rose.

Thabiti looked up and grinned sheepishly. "He is, but we think your need is greater than his, and it might be just the excuse we need to persuade him to leave. He doesn't appear to be making any attempt to find alternative accommodation, and if we're not careful, he'll become a permanent fixture."

Rose reached out and touched Thabiti's arm. "That's very kind of you both, although I'd have to look for somewhere else to keep my animals."

"I'm afraid we can't help you with them, but I'm sure someone would be willing to lend you a field and I could help build a shelter. Is your car open?"

"I'll just fetch the keys."

Rose returned and handed her car keys to Thabiti. She said, "Hellen Newton came back to see me. She's spoken to my landlord and persuaded him to let me stay for at least another month. In fact, she said a sale might take several months to complete. So that's a relief."

Thabiti stopped and looked over at Rose's colourful garden and Mount Kenya rising proudly beyond it. "This is a lovely property. But if his daughter wants to live in Nairobi, it'll be expensive to buy her a house. But I would have expected him to keep the field as it's a great investment opportunity for a future housing estate."

Rose shivered, "New houses packed together on my field. Sorry, I know it's not mine, but I love watching my animals grazing and I can't bear to think of it being covered in concrete. And they'll probably chop down the wonderful Cape Chestnut tree."

Thabiti swallowed and replied, "I know, but I watched it happen in Nairobi. It's only a matter of time before this area is developed. Consider how many new blocks of flats are being constructed in the centre of town."

He walked across to the wooden garage and unlocked Rose's car. He opened the passenger door and leaned inside.

When he reappeared he said, "When I've finished here, I'm driving to Nyeri. The plane hunting expedition is tomorrow." He removed the plastic packaging from the air filter and disappeared back inside the car.

Rose realised she was going to Samburu the following day for the Great Grevy's Rally. She felt her chest tighten as she looked from the field, to the stables, to her cottage. She wished she hadn't agreed to join Chloe as she'd rather spend the weekend at home.

Thabiti resurfaced again. "Pearl is excited about your girls' trip to Samburu this weekend." He grinned. "I just hope you don't feel left out as she and Chloe are becoming firm friends."

"I'm glad about that," mused Rose. "They've both had their issues recently, so they should be able to help each other."

Thabiti returned to his work.

CHAPTER TWENTY-FOUR

Thabiti drove the Land Cruiser, which had belonged to his mother, up the final steep hill, and past the prestigious Mount Kenya Academy, on the way to Nyeri.

The town of Nyeri was located sixty kilometres south of Nanyuki, towards Nairobi. It was the former administrative headquarters for Kenya's Central Province and was a fertile agricultural area, lying to the east of the Aberdare Range and to the west of Mount Kenya.

Internationally it was famous for being the final resting place of Robert Baden-Powell, the founder of the Scout movement.

Thabiti knew it best as being one of the major areas for the Kikuyu tribe, which he was part of, and the hometown of his mother's mentor and friend, Wangari Maathai.

Wangari had been a member of parliament, where she served as assistant minister for the environment and natural resources. But Thabiti remembered his mother talking about her as the 'tree lady'.

"Wangari set up the Green Belt Movement, an environmental organisation which focused on planting trees. For this, and her work promoting women's rights, she became the first African woman to be awarded the Nobel Peace Prize. An achievement his mother had been very proud of.

Thabiti stopped by a wooden hut displaying a red Coca Cola sign. He wound down the passenger window and called to the shopkeeper, "Habari. Where is the new brewery and bottling plant being built?"

"You won't be able to visit it. It can only be accessed through another plot, which is located just past the tea estate," the shopkeeper replied and returned to his duka.

Thabiti drove alongside a neatly trimmed hedge of duranta. A sign beside an impressive entrance gate announced 'Kenya Chai Producers Limited'. After another half a mile, the well-maintained hedge was replaced by one which was unruly and full of weeds.

Thabiti pulled off the road. He got out of the car and leaned against a metal five-bar gate, looking at the land beyond it. There was a track, along the left-hand side, which looked well used and someone had recently laid a fresh layer of gravel.

But the rest of the property looked unkempt with either bare patches of earth or clumps of scraggy bushes. He spotted the tiled roof of a house at the top of an incline, surround by jacaranda and flame trees.

A thin-looking horse wandered towards him, shaking its head to try to ward off flies. It nudged his arm with its muzzle.

Gingerly, he stroked its face. "You look hungry, but I'm afraid I don't have any food for you."

"They don't know how to look after their animals or their land." Thabiti jumped and the horse turned and trotted back to join its friend.

An old African man with leathery skin shuffled across to stand beside the gate. He leaned on his stick and asked, "Are you lost young man or are you visiting?"

Thabiti turned to the stranger and said, "I was looking for the site of the proposed new brewery."

The old man lifted his stick and pointed down the track. "It's at the end of this, behind that house. Lots of vehicles have been driving up and down recently, but I don't think they'll take kindly to strangers snooping around."

Thabiti's face fell.

The old man leaned on his stick again and asked, "What's your interest in it?"

"I'd read about the hydro-electric dam they are proposing to build and the environmentally friendly method of dealing with their wastewater and other products."

The old man shook his head. "I don't know much about that, but they're disturbing the ghosts of my ancestors."

Thabiti looked at him dubiously. "What do you mean?"

"I can feel their unsettled spirits. It led to death last time." He paused, gazed into the distance, and then bowed his shaking head. "And it has done so again."

Thabiti felt a chill run down his spine. Was this old man trying to scare him away? He asked, "Do you live here?"

The old man looked up at him and Thabiti caught his breath, so intense were the man's eyes. "No, not anymore. But this is my ancestral land, and a curse on anyone who disturbs it."

CHAPTER TWENTY-FIVE

Thabiti sat in the back of Pete Stephenson's Land Cruiser outside the Outspan Hotel in Nyeri.

Pete leaned in and said, "We're just waiting for Otto. I made sure he was awake before I came down, but he arrived quite late last night, after playing polo chukkas at the new ground in Timau. I warned him against driving here in the dark, but he ignored me."

A young man with unruly, fair, curly hair climbed in beside Thabiti and murmured, "Sorry." The laces of his boots hung loose and he carried his coat, hat and a small rucksack.

"That's everyone," Pete shouted across to the driver of the second vehicle. A tall African man climbed into the passenger seat as Pete turned on the ignition and they drove out of the hotel entrance.

Otto finished tying the laces of his boots and looked up at Thabiti. "Hello again. Sorry to keep you waiting. Pete says you'll be filming any wreckage he finds."

"That's right," replied Thabiti, as he pulled his own black rucksack towards him.

Pete called through from the front, "Why do you think you might find the Munros' plane near the Blenheim bomber wreckage?"

Otto leaned forward between the front seats and explained, "There's a large area of bamboo nearby which could have easily hidden a light aircraft. And apparently the fire on the moor also damaged it. I've no idea if the plane is there, but I thought this was too good an opportunity to miss."

Thabiti muttered to himself, "Munro. Wasn't that the name of the woman who died at the Bushman's Restaurant?"

Otto must have heard him as he sat back and turned to Thabiti. "Becky Munro. Her parents disappeared over nine years ago, flying back to Nyeri from Nairobi. Their plane was never found, and neither were they.

"Becky and Eloise applied to the Kenyan court to declare their parents legally dead, so they can sort out the estate, but the court has been reticent about doing so. I thought I could help Becky if I found her parents' bodies." He turned to the window. "But even if I do, it's too late now."

Thabiti watched Otto, whose shoulders shook. Thabiti looked away and swallowed. His thoughts drifted to Marina. Was she enjoying helping the refugees at Kakuma Camp?

Would she want to become a permanent charity worker, and travel the world helping different groups of people as they struggled to survive? Would Nanyuki become too small and sedentary for her? Would she want a more exciting life with more stimulating people? People other than him.

He was drawn back to Otto and asked in a hushed voice, "Was she important to you?"

Otto turned his red, puffy face to Thabiti and nodded.

"She was my world. We were so happy growing up. I spent many wonderful days with her and her family at Roho House, just outside Nyeri. My father was one of the managers at the neighbouring tea estate which her family, and Guy Ramsey's, used to own. I thought her time in England was just to get over her parents' disappearance, and that she'd come back to Kenya. Return to me." Otto wiped his eyes.

Thabiti was surprised to feel an ache in his chest along with the image of Marina in his mind.

Otto declared, "But she said she couldn't. That she was marrying someone else."

The car turned off the tarmac road onto a track heading towards the Aberdare Forest. Thabiti and Otto were silent for several minutes.

Then Otto turned to Thabiti and confided, "The last words I spoke to her were in anger." He sniffed. "I wanted to talk to her again at the Bushman's Restaurant but I didn't get a chance."

Thabiti flinched. "You were at the Bushman's on Saturday, when she collapsed?"

"Yes. I'd been splashing my face with cold water to calm myself down and as I walked towards Becky, she started dancing. Then someone threw something and she fell down. Eloise screamed and I bottled it and kept on walking out of the bottom gate. If I'd known that was the last I'd see of her ..."

He gulped and turned back to the window.

CHAPTER TWENTY-SIX

The large trees and dense vegetation of the Aberdare Forest gave way to bushes and the occasional eucalyptus tree as Pete Stephenson drove along a dirt track which wound its way ever upwards.

Thabiti looked out of the car window as they left the forest behind and emerged onto open moorland. They drove past a small pond surrounded by tufts of various different grasses and small leafy bushes.

Pete said, "This area reminds me of Scotland with its thistles, large expanses of giant heather and wild flowers. But local people talk about an albino zebra."

Pete pulled to stop as the terrain changed again. Large expanses of rock rose above them, and the stony ground was covered in plants rather than grass. Thabiti thought the small cactus trees gave the area an eerie feeling.

Pete said, "We'll have to walk the rest of the way," Pete announced.

Thabiti pulled himself up onto another rocky outcrop and saw more moorland spread before him. He had no idea that such a surreal landscape existed. He'd driven around the fringes of the Aberdare Range before, but thought it was completely covered in trees and forest. This area felt untouched since the time of creation.

After an hour's climb, Pete stopped and pointed, "Look at that darker area. It's where the fire was."

They headed towards the burnt area.

"Not far now," Pete called. "I can see the hill where we found the wreckage. And Otto was right, the bamboo forest to the north has also been damaged by the fire."

They continued their ascent.

Thabiti scrambled up to join Pete and Otto on the brow of a hill and saw large rusty pieces of metal spread out before them. He pulled out his camera and began recording.

Pete explained, "Here we have some wreckage from a Blenheim bomber. This is part of the undercarriage housing." He moved across to a straight piece of metal, "And this is the leading edge of a wing."

He stood up and said, "And there are rusty gears and springs scattered all around. Today we're looking for the engine, or any parts of the fuselage which will identify the aircraft."

Thabiti put his camera down.

Pete suggested, "Why not film some of the guys as they continue their search?"

Otto said, "I'm going to check out the bamboo forest."

There was a shout from the tall African man who had travelled in the car with them. Pete and Thabiti rushed to join him and Thabiti filmed as Pete carefully extracted a long, round, rusty object from amongst the burnt undergrowth.

Pete held it up with pride. "This is the remains of a .303 machine gun."

There was another shout, from searchers a hundred metres the other side of the main wreckage.

When they reached the team from the other car, Pete drew in his breath and looked down at two large round chunks of metal, one of which had a number of protrusions extending from it. He cried, "Well done, these are the nine-cylinder air-cooled radial engines. And one's in reasonable condition."

Thabiti filmed as Pete knelt by the least rusty engine block and began scraping at it with his penknife. "I think I've found something." He scraped more urgently and exclaimed, "It's the engine plate and number. We can finally identify the plane this wreckage belongs to."

Otto joined them. He was panting and between breaths gasped, "I've found something."

Pete, Thabiti, and the tall African man, followed Otto towards the bamboo forest. Although part of it had been burnt it was still very thick and they had to fight their way along a narrow path which Otto had created.

Otto stepped to one side and announced, "Look, I think that's a tail fin."

Pete stepped forward and said, "I believe you're right."

The tall African man pushed past them and raised his machete. He began to hack at the thick undergrowth. The white-coloured fuselage of a small plane was slowly revealed, together with its registration number written in red lettering: 5Y-VAT.

Otto sank to his knees. "This is it. This is Michael Munro's plane."

CHAPTER TWENTY-SEVEN

On Friday evening Rose followed Chloe and Pearl through the entrance and up the ramp to the reception area of Punda Milia Lodge. Chloe had driven them the two hours from Nanyuki to the lodge, which was located to the north-east of Nanyuki, in Samburu National Reserve.

Rose placed her canvas overnight bag on the ground as two waiters approached. One carried a metal tray with glasses of fruit juice, and the other a basket of warm face towels.

"Wonderful," declared Chloe as she patted her face. "But I think I'll pass on the juice. That last stretch was exhausting to drive. You'd think the council would do something about the road considering the prices they charge to enter the reserve." She placed her towel in an empty basket and said to the waiter, "Can I have a gin and tonic, please."

She removed an envelope from her bag and patted Rose's arm. "Why don't you grab a seat whilst Pearl and I check in."

Chloe and Pearl turned and joined a small queue in front of the reception desk.

Rose walked across to the far side of the reception area and leaned against a rail. She had a clear view down to the Ewaso Nyiro River. A troop of baboons were sitting beside a doum palm, and younger members were racing up and down its trunk.

The reception was busy with guests, whom she presumed were mostly involved in the Great Grevy's Rally.

She recognised the oily voice of Fergus Peacock, the lawyer. "Tessa, you know that Alex and Guy have run their business into the ground. Alex does what he can but he's pretty hopeless, and Guy prefers to swan around rather than do any actual work. They've invested a fortune in an upmarket mobile safari camp but they're not marketing it to the right clients."

Tessa replied tartly, "What has my brother's safari business to do with you."

Fergus responded nonchalantly, "Nothing, I just thought you'd like to know. But if you're not bothered who takes the company over, I'll take my leave."

"What are you talking about? The business isn't up for sale." Tessa's voice was tense.

"Not officially. But it is in trouble, and Eloise is prepared to bail Alex and Guy out," needled Fergus.

"Well, that's no surprise. It's a badly kept secret that Guy used her money to buy into the business in the first place."

"But this isn't for Guy." Rose strained to hear the rest of the conversation as Fergus lowered his voice. "Eloise will only provide the money if she can buy the remaining shares and run the company."

Tessa gasped. "I don't believe you."

Rose turned and watched Guy and Eloise approach Tessa and Fergus.

Guy remarked, "What poison are you dripping now?"

Fergus ignored the remark, smiled at Eloise and said, "I'll bid you good night and see you in the morning."

"Where are you going?" Eloise asked in a perplexed tone.

"Koitogor Lodge. You don't think I'd stay here do you?" He strode away. Tessa, Guy and Eloise watched him leave before they too exited the reception area.

Chloe and Pearl joined Rose. "Here's your key." She handed Rose a piece of wood with Room 5 etched into it before waving to a waiter to catch his attention. "And here is my G and T." She sipped appreciatively.

CHAPTER TWENTY-EIGHT

Rose stood beside Chloe's Land Cruiser, which was parked in front of Punda Milia Lodge. She stamped her feet in the chill, early morning air and, despite wearing a pair of compression gloves, her arthritic fingers throbbed. She tried wriggling them to aid the circulation but only her fingertips moved.

Chloe and Pearl carried cool boxes and baskets from the lodge and packed them into the back of the car. "That's the last one," announced Chloe as she strained under the weight of a large blue cool box.

"I can't believe I'm up and it's still dark," remarked Pearl. "Before the yoga retreat on Borana, I'd never even seen sunrise."

Chloe reached inside a basket and removed a vacuum flask. "I'm so glad the lodge left this outside my room. I've brought it with me as I only managed half a cup of coffee earlier." She unscrewed the top and poured steaming liquid into the lid. She offered it to Rose.

"No, thank you. I've already had some tea." Rose continued to flex her stiff fingers.

Pearl grinned, "Thabiti will be sorry to miss out on the breakfast the lodge has packed for us."

"And they've provided lunch. No wonder there were so many bags." Chloe clasped the lid of the flask in both hands and sipped from it.

There was a clap of hands. Around the parking area groups of people, standing by various 4x4s, ceased their conversations. Gabriel Baker, with his sleek shoulder-length hair, held up his hand. Despite the cold morning he wore tan-coloured shorts and a fleece with a zebra motif.

He said in a hoarse voice, "Welcome everyone to the first Great Grevy's Rally."

"Speak up, we can't hear you," a man called from behind Rose.

Gabriel coughed and shouted, "Good morning, everyone."

There was a dull mutter of responses.

Gabriel continued, "Each team should have an information pack and a GPS-enabled camera."

Chloe reached into her basket again and extracted a white cardboard folder and black camera case.

"Some of you have also been allocated a Kenya Wildlife officer to assist you. But first, can a member of each team come over and collect your goodie bags."

Chloe nudge Pearl. "You go."

Pearl returned with five black-and-white striped cotton bags. "They've given us some extra ones, so I might keep one for Thabiti."

Chloe grinned, "He'll be happy, especially if there's food inside."

Gabriel shouted above the murmur of conversations. "Thank you for volunteering to help this important conservation initiative. Media attention on the loss of African wildlife is welcome, but it concentrates on elephants and rhino.

"We, at the Grevy's Zebra Trust, estimate the Grevy's population has declined by over eighty per cent in the past fifty years, but we can't prove it. That's why your help over the next two days is vital as we record individual Grevy's. Inside your information pack is a map of your group's census area."

Chloe opened the information pack and withdrew an A4-sized coloured map. She held it up for Rose to see.

"Sorry, my glasses are in the car," admitted Rose.

Pearl joined Chloe and said, "Our search area starts halfway between this lodge and the recently reconstructed bridge over the Ewaso Nyiro River."

"Just a few more minutes, please," Gabriel shouted. "Instructions on using your camera to record each Grevy are provided in your folder.

Just remember, you are to photograph the right-hand side of the zebra."

A voice from the audience asked, "What happens if we photograph a zebra more than once."

Gabriel held up his hand for silence. "Good question. Our US analysts have developed stripe recognition software, so they can discount multiple photos of the same animal. Now it's time to leave. The census starts at seven thirty and you need to be in your search area by then. Good luck and happy snapping."

A Safari Land Cruiser was parked a few metres from Chloe's car. It was a heavy utilitarian vehicle with canvas sides, which rolled up for improved game-viewing. Rose heard arguing as Guy and Eloise Ramsey emerged at the rear of the vehicle.

"Guy, I am not driving this beast." Eloise tucked a strand of errant hair behind her ear.

"Why not? I promised Alex I'd introduce him to my Samburu contact this morning."

"But you've had all week to do that. This weekend was supposed to be special. To be family time." She burst into tears. Guy gingerly put his arms around his wife as he looked about the car park.

Rose stepped out of sight behind Chloe's car.

She heard Alex Newton call, "So sorry I'm late. Mia woke up and she's very upset about not being able to join us. So Hellen's decided to stay with her and Liam and take them to the pool. Are you all right, Eloise?"

Eloise turned away from Guy's loose embrace and wiped her eyes.

Tessa strode to join them. She looked around the group and remarked, "I can see everyone's raring to go."

Guy dangled a set of car keys in front of her. "You can drive, Tessa."

She smirked at him. "Not a chance. I'm on holiday." She climbed into the back of the safari vehicle.

"Morning all," drawled a deep voice behind Rose.

She started in surprise and turned to face Sam Mwamba, Constable Wachira's significantly larger other half, standing by Chloe's Land Cruiser.

He approached Rose and stared past her. "Who were you watching?"

She turned back towards the group as Alex Newton lifted bags into the safari vehicle's front row of seats. Alex asked, "Where's Fergus?"

"Not here yet," replied Guy.

Eloise quipped, "Typical Fergus, thinking that he's better than the rest of us."

"Of course, it's got nothing to do with a group of poker players who are staying at the Koitogor Lodge," Tessa called down.

Alex's face lit up as he remarked, "Really?"

Tessa laughed sarcastically. "He didn't tell you? A good job as Hellen would murder you."

"Sam," cried Chloe.

Sam and Rose turned and joined Chloe and Pearl by the car.

Chloe was beaming. "What are you doing here?"

"I'm your KWS officer. I'll be helping you with the census."

"That's great," added Rose, but she looked around uneasily. Recently, it seemed there was trouble at any event both she and Sam attended.

Chloe started the car and Rose climbed into the back beside Pearl. The blue uniformed guard at the exit of Punda Milia Lodge, raised the barrier and they drove out into Samburu National Reserve.

CHAPTER TWENTY-NINE

C hloe turned left out of Punda Milia Lodge onto a red volcanic soil track.

Sam whispered, "Steady. Look ahead."

Through the strengthening light they spotted a small fox-like creature with a black striped back. "Its mate should join it soon."

Sure enough, a second jackal emerged from the long dry grass adjacent to the track and the pair trotted away. "Black-backed jackals. They mate for life and work together hunting and marking their territorial boundaries."

Pearl reached for her phone. Then put it down. "It's too dark to take photos."

They drove to the far end of their census area which was marked by a large concrete bridge.

"This bridge is rather industrial for a wildlife reserve. I expected a small wooden structure," remarked Chloe.

"The last bridge was washed away in a flood, together with a number of safari camps," responded Rose. "Why don't you drive across? Buffalo Springs National Reserve is on the far side."

As they drove along the bridge, Rose glanced down at the Ewaso Nyiro River far below.

At the far end Chloe pointed to her right and asked, "Who are those people?" There was a cluster of low round huts with dung or wooden-slatted sides and animal hide roofs. Long-legged sheep and goats, and thin looking cattle, clustered around a central watering point.

"Samburu tribesmen," replied Sam. "They used to roam across wide areas of Samburu County, up to the Mathews Range, but their access has been restricted. So instead they've settled in small villages. This one has a permanent spring for them and their livestock, but it means the wild animals can't use it. Competition with livestock for water is a big reason for the decline in Grevy's zebra numbers."

It was ten past seven when Chloe drove back over the bridge and turned right into their census area. They rounded a corner and the Ewaso Nyiro riverbed stretched before them. It was wide, perhaps fifty metres across in places, but the river itself was confined to the middle third of the riverbed.

"The river's drying up," observed Rose.

Sam confirmed, "Yes, it's several months since there was rain on Mount Kenya and the Aberdare Range which are the river's sources. It'll drop to a trickle unless the short rains arrive early this year."

Beside Rose, Pearl gasped. On the river bank, in front of them, a small herd of elephants gathered. Two larger animals lumbered forward onto the dry riverbed, which was cracked to create a crazy-paving effect, and the rest of the group followed.

"I need a photo," exclaimed Chloe. They watched as the elephants reached the water's edge and began to drink.

"As elephants are so large they need lots of water to stay hydrated," explained Sam. "And they can drink up to fifty gallons a day, which is the same as drinking a bathtub's worth of water."

Another larger herd appeared on the far bank.

"More elephants," Chloe cried. She opened the passenger door and stood on her Land Cruiser's running board to take photographs.

"It's the dry season, so the elephants are leaving the arid northern areas of Kenya in search of food and water. Although they can last four days without water, they are attracted to the Samburu and Buffalo Springs area because of the river."

Pearl commented, "The elephants appear more red than grey in colour."

"That's from the red Samburu soil which covers them," replied Sam.

Chloe climbed back into the car and drove on.

"Are you ready to start the census?" asked Sam. "It's nearly seven thirty."

Pearl was in charge of the survey camera. She opened the information pack and said, "Our instructions are to photograph only the right-hand side of each zebra?"

Sam replied, "Yes, otherwise we'll confuse the analysts. And the camera is GPS enabled so they can determine the location of each zebra when its picture was taken. "

"That makes sense," said Pearl, placing the camera on the seat between her and Rose.

"Look!" exclaimed Chloe. "There's a herd of zebra."

Sam turned to her and said, "I'm afraid they're not Grevy's. Those are Burchell's zebra, a sub-species of plains zebra. Although their numbers are declining, and they are considered 'near threatened', they're quite common in Kenya. And far more so than their cousins, the Grevy's."

"Can I suggest we turn away from the river?" said Rose.

"Of course." Chloe turned north at the next track and Ol Olokwe, a slab of mountain some twenty-five miles away, stood out clearly in the distance.

The peace was shattered by a buzzing noise emanating from Rose's bag, which lay at her feet. She felt the colour rising in her cheeks as she apologised, "Sorry, I forgot to turn my phone off. Do you mind if I take this call?" She fished inside her bag and answered her phone.

A female voice asked, "Is that Rose Hardie?"

"Yes," said Rose uncertainly. She didn't recognise the voice.

"I've been told that you're in Samburu taking part in the Great Grevy's Rally."

"That's correct." Rose was still hesitant.

Chloe slowed to a stop.

"I need your help. We've been brought an abandoned Grevy's foal but it won't drink, and I'm worried that it won't survive. I know you're participating in the census, but can you come and help us? After all, preserving the life of Grevy's is what the initiative is all about."

Rose asked, "Who, and where are you?"

"The Ivory Impact Initiative camp, a kilometre or so north of the bridge. I'm Ellen, by the way."

CHAPTER THIRTY

C hloe drove through a gateway, between thornbush fences, into a red soil yard. She parked in front of a tall, open-sided wooden structure with chairs and tables visible within. Behind it were a number of permanent-looking canvas tents.

A young woman with unruly curly hair escaping from a makeshift bun greeted them. "I'm Ellen. Thank you for coming." She turned towards the tents and called, "John."

A tall, imperial African tribesman appeared. He wore a red-checked shuka blanket wrapped around his waist but otherwise he was naked, except for an impressive collection of bead necklaces and two gold hooped earrings.

Ellen asked, "Please can you give our visitors some refreshments. Rose, if you'll follow me."

Pearl and Chloe followed John but Sam accompanied Rose.

They found the zebra foal outside a tan-coloured tent which looked as if it was used as an office. The foal was waist height and all legs and fluffy ears.

"I couldn't get it to drink water and it's refusing milk," explained Ellen.

Rose approached the foal, but it shied away from her. "I'd say it's less than three months old, so it won't drink water yet. But milk should be fine. What type are you using?"

"Cow's milk," replied Ellen.

"Good, but it'll need some extra nutrients. Add two tablespoons of glucose or brown sugar to the next bottle and, if you have any, six drops of cod liver oil."

Sam reached for the milk bottle, which was actually a recycled two-litre plastic Fanta bottle.

A brown teat had been secured to the end with an elastic band. Sam held the bottle out, inviting the foal. It staggered forward and licked the teat, but it did not latch on.

Rose smiled at the sight of Sam, a giant of a man, squatting on the dry earth as he tried to coax the fragile young zebra.

"Come on, just take hold of it," he encouraged, pointing the teat towards the foal.

"Where did you find the foal?" Rose asked.

"A couple of rangers brought it to us this morning in the back of their pickup. They found it alone, beside one of the tracks, with no adult zebra in sight."

Sam looked up. "Unlike horses and Burchell's zebra, Grevy's foals don't always follow their mothers to water. They are often left with another adult."

"So I guess this one was separated from its minder." Rose continued to watch Sam, but the foal appeared uncertain and unable to latch onto the teat. She was reminded of a story Craig had once told her. When visiting a friend, he was surprised to witness a zebra foal standing behind his friend's wife, nuzzling between her legs.

"She explained that the foal would only drink from a bottle placed backwards between her thighs. She presumed it needed the security and comfort of darkness for its eyes and nose, and that its face needed to be pressed against something warm.

"Can I try?" Rose asked, moving cautiously towards Sam.

He handed her the bottle and she turned away from the foal and secured the bottle between her thighs, with the teat facing backwards.

Sam whispered, "What are you doing?"

"Shush, I'm trying something I remember Craig telling me about."

They waited as the zebra foal took nervous steps towards Rose. Its muzzle snuffled against her legs and butted her bottom. Rose was tall, lanky and strong for her age, but no match for a hungry zebra. Sam jumped up and supported Rose as the zebra latched onto the bottle.

Ellen rearranged her hair. "I'd never have thought of doing it that way."

After several minutes, the zebra raised and shook its head. It wandered over to the thorn bush fence.

Sam let go of Rose and asked, "Are you all right?"

Rose removed the bottle from between her legs. "I am now." She turned and watched the foal. "Zebra really are amazing creatures. We'll never know just how and why they developed their striped hide."

Chloe and Pearl joined them, and Chloe handed Rose a mug. "I've brought you some tea."

"Thank you. And Pearl, we need to take a photo of this foal. Our first Grevy's sighting."

CHAPTER THIRTY-ONE

Rose and her companions continued their census work and as time passed the heat of the day intensified.

Chloe drove through an arid landscape with swaying fronds of yellow grass, and small clumps of thorn bushes. "Oh, look at the man," she cried. "He's like a Maasai warrior from a tourist brochure, with his bare chest, red shuka, and his head and neck adorned in beadwork."

"A Samburu tribesman," noted Sam.

Pearl leaned forward and asked, "What's he doing?"

Chloe added, "And what's that funny looking plant? It reminds me of a large bulb of fennel, but with pink flowers."

"That's a desert rose," said Sam, "And it looks like he's removing part of the stem."

They watched the tribesman squat on his haunches by the plant and hack at its base.

Chloe drove on along a track which meandered towards the river, and then turned and continued parallel with it. She said, "I think I'm starting to get my bearings. That green corridor, with the tall trees, is the river."

"Yes, and the trees are doum palms," said Sam.

"So what's the huge pyramid-shaped hill over there?"

Sam replied, "That's Koitogor, it's part of a ridge which runs north to south through the reserve, and at this angle it looks triangular in shape."

Chloe continued to drive slowly around their census area. They spotted several herds of impala and some Grant's gazelle, with their white bottoms and long curved horns.

"Where are the Grevy's zebra?" Pearl grumbled. She yawned and leaned against the car window.

Rose consoled her, "I guess if they were around every corner we wouldn't need to conduct this census. But it is getting rather monotonous. Shall we find somewhere in the shade for lunch?"

Sam agreed, "We might as well. It's past midday and most of the animals will be sleeping. I know somewhere by the river where we can have our picnic."

Chloe followed Sam's directions until he suddenly announced, "Stop."

She braked sharply and queried, "Surely we're not having lunch here?"

He pointed towards a solitary acacia tree. "Look, a Grevy's zebra."

Chloe leaned forward and watched the zebra standing under the shade of the tree. "How can you tell it's not one of the other types?"

"It's much larger for a start, with round, cartoon-mouse style ears. And its stripes are much narrower," explained Sam.

Pearl removed the camera from its case and opened the door.

"Careful," said Sam also getting out of the car. "We'll need to walk in a wide circle so as to photograph its right-hand side without scaring it away."

Chloe drove into a clearing next to the river. A Safari Land Cruiser was parked on the far side. "Shall we find somewhere else?" she asked.

Pearl had been dozing. She opened her eyes and urged, "Can't we just stay here?"

Sam peered through the windscreen. "Isn't that the group you were listening in to this morning, Mama Rose? The ones who were also at the Bushman's Restaurant last Saturday with the woman who died."

Rose stiffened. "I was observing them." She watched Alex Newton lift a basket out of the safari vehicle. "Yes, that's them. Shall I ask if they mind sharing this picnic spot with us?"

As she climbed out of the car she watched Guy Ramsey and Fergus Peacock walk towards the river. Fergus offered Guy a small bottle but he shook his head and took a swig from a can of beer.

Rose strode across the sandy ground. She heard a high-pitched call and a group of vulture guinea fowl ran out from behind a bush. Their bright blue bellies contrasted with their black and white backs and their long slender necks.

As she drew closer, she realised Guy and Fergus were arguing. They tried to keep their voices hushed but occasional words reached Rose like, "No" and "Not my fault," and "Sort it out yourself."

Tessa was arranging food on a small table. She looked up at Rose and said, "Yes, can we help you?"

Rose bristled. "There's no need to take that tone with me. I only wanted to ask if you minded us setting up our lunch under that tree?" Rose pointed at the large gnarled trunk of the wild fig tree beside which Chloe had parked.

Alex stepped forward. "Please ignore my sister. Of course we don't mind."

Tessa turned away and removed plates and cutlery from a basket.

Eloise removed her sunglasses and Rose noted her bloodshot eyes. "You were the one who tried to help my sister when she collapsed?"

"Yes, I'm sorry I couldn't prevent her ..." Rose couldn't bring herself to say 'dying' as she saw Eloise's eyes fill with tears.

Alex placed his arm around Eloise and said to Rose, "We appreciate you trying. I presume you're part of the Grevy's Rally. How was your search this morning?"

"Not very successful," admitted Rose. "We did record two Grevy's but one was an abandoned foal at a conservation camp. What about yourselves? Did you have a fruitful morning?"

Eloise shook off Alex's arm and said dismissively, "It was a complete waste of time. Alex got this beast of a car stuck in sand and we had to wait for a passing tourist vehicle to pull us out." She sat down heavily in a canvas safari chair.

Alex replied patiently, "I did tell Fergus there was no point taking that shortcut."

Guy and Fergus rejoined the group. They ignored Rose, and Guy helped himself to another beer from the cool box.

"Are you making drinks?" Eloise called.

Guy turned away from Fergus and replied, "Yes. What would you like? G and T or a glass of wine?"

"I'd like some tea, please. There should be some mint and lemon verbena sachets in the basket."

Alex came and stood beside Rose. He said, "We did spot one Grevy's, and a couple of lions as we drove along the river bank."

Guy handed a mug to Tessa. "Give this to Eloise?" He turned his back on her, and he and Fergus stepped away from the group again.

Tessa rolled her eyes as she handed the mug to Eloise and said, "I'm hungry. Even if the rest of you can't be bothered, I'm going to have lunch."

Eloise sipped her tea. She screwed up her eyes, looked at her mug and took another sip.

Alex turned to Eloise and asked, "Can I get you anything to eat?"

Rose's mouth felt dry and she coughed. "I hope your afternoon is more successful." Not receiving a response, she turned and walked back across the clearing with an unsettled feeling.

Sam was unfolding chairs and Chloe and Pearl were removing plastic Tupperware boxes and aluminium foil packages from the cool boxes.

Chloe remarked, "We presumed it was OK to start preparing lunch."

Rose replied, "Good idea. I'm suddenly rather hungry."

CHAPTER THIRTY-TWO

I t was six o'clock on Saturday evening when Rose and her group returned to Punda Milia Lodge.

Sam said, "I'm going to check in with Gabriel and the Grevy's Rally team. Shall I meet you later for supper?"

Chloe nodded and suggested, "Shall we say seven o'clock at the bar?" She and Pearl left for their rooms.

Rose wandered through the main reception area, where Alex Newton was talking to the receptionist, and out onto a viewing deck by the swimming pool.

She was not the only one who'd decided to have a drink by the pool. Hellen Newton was sitting with her children, who were having their tea. Alex joined them and kissed Hellen on the lips.

Hellen commented, "You've had a long day."

The toddler Liam picked up his bottle and threw it on the floor. Hellen sighed and leaned down to pick it up.

"And I'm not the only one by the looks of it. But I've confirmed with reception that they'll send someone to babysit at seven. Then we can enjoy a relaxing evening together."

A waiter approached Rose and asked, "Can I get you anything?"

She looked at him gratefully and replied, "A Kericho Gold tea please." He nodded and left.

Tessa Newton and Eloise Ramsey were sitting at another table. Eloise stood up and walked across to speak with Hellen. Tessa removed something from her bag, looked around furtively and bent over the table. Rose wondered what she was up to.

Guy Ramsey sauntered onto the deck and stood by his wife. He said, "Fergus has agreed to grace us with his presence for supper. He's returned to his lodge to change but promised to be back by a quarter past seven."

"If he's not, I won't be waiting for him." Eloise rejoined Tessa. She sipped her drink, grimaced and exclaimed, "What's wrong with me? Everything I drink today tastes bitter."

"Here, give it a stir."

Eloise stirred her drink and took another sip. "That's better. Oh, look at that elephant."

Rose looked towards the river as a lone bull elephant wandered past on the other side of the fence, swaying its trunk back and forth.

Rose sank into the zebra-patterned cushions in Punda Milia's bar and realised she'd eaten too much for supper. It was her own fault. Why had she needed to taste two puddings?

Sam, Chloe and Pearl joined her.

"Coffee anyone?" Chloe asked, "Or something stronger?"

Rose shook her head. "Nothing for me, thank you. I'm going to bed soon. We've another early start in the morning."

Sam sat down and opened a large oval-shaped wooden box. "Can I have a Tusker?"

Pearl sat down opposite Sam. "Nothing for me, thank you."

Chloe strode across to the bar.

Pearl leaned forward and touched the inside of the box. There were two rows of six indentations and two larger holes at each end. "I've seen one of these before. Is it a game?"

Sam picked up some coloured stones and replied, "It's a mancala board. Do you want to play?"

Pearl shook her head and sat back.

Chloe sat next to her and said enthusiastically, "I will. What do I have to do?"

Sam opened his large hand, revealing the coloured stones. "I'll place four of these in each cavity." He placed the stones in the holes in the board. "To start the game, choose one hole and pick up all the stones in it."

Chloe followed Sam's instructions.

Sam continued, "Now drop one stone in each of the next four holes."

Chloe placed three stones in holes and held up the final stone. "Do I put this one in the large hole at the end?"

"Yes, that one's the mancala, and because you've put a stone in it, you get another go."

Pearl tilted her head and watched them. "Are you sure you're not making this up?"

"Aagh!"

Rose looked up. Eloise Ramsey grabbed hold of the door frame and then doubled over.

Hellen Newton rushed over to support her and asked, "Is it your stomach again?"

"Yes, it's cramping." Eloise spoke through gritted teeth. "I must have eaten something which disagreed with me."

"Sit here." Hellen guided Eloise to an empty chair. "I'll go and ask reception to contact a doctor."

Chloe stared at the mancala board and asked, "Why have you taken all my stones?"

Sam replied, "Because I placed my last stone in an empty cavity, I get to take all the stones in the opposite one."

Chloe shook her head. "I don't get it."

Hellen returned. "No luck with a doctor I'm afraid. The hotel can call Amref, but they won't fly until it's light. Shall I have a look in my first aid kit? I might have something to ease your pain."

Rose stood and joined Hellen and Eloise. "Can I help? I'm not a doctor but I have some medical experience, although it's mostly with animals."

Eloise pinched her mouth. "You're a vet? I'm not sure how you can help me."

Hellen asked, "Is there anything we can give her to ease the pain?"

"You could try Imodium or Pepto-Bismal if you have any. But she'll probably get the most relief from curling up in bed with a hot water bottle."

Eloise looked at Rose and smiled wistfully. "Yes, a hot water bottle."

Hellen stood and helped Eloise to her feet. "Let's get you to your room, and then I'll find one for you."

Eloise grabbed Hellen for support and murmured, "I'm sorry to spoil your evening. Especially as you were having some time away from the kids."

"Don't worry," murmured Hellen.

CHAPTER THIRTY-THREE

R ose heard banging and a voice shouted, "Daktari."

She rubbed her eyes as the banging continued.

"Just a minute," she called.

Opening the door of her room, she found a young man wearing the hotel uniform. He bobbed up and down and blurted, "Quick, Quick. Memsaab need you."

Rose closed the door and quickly pulled on trousers, shoes and a jacket. She flexed her fingers to encourage circulation.

She hurried after the young man, through the dimly lit central hotel area, to a room where the door stood ajar. Stepping inside, she saw Eloise Ramsey lying in bed. Hellen was seated by the bed and her face looked grey. In contrast, Eloise's skin was red, but she was not sweating.

"Is her stomach still cramping?" asked Rose.

"Yes, and more frequently and severe. And she complained that she felt dizzy." Hellen's eyes were wide and her voice sounded as brittle as a dry twig. "What can we do?

Rose leaned over Eloise and asked, "Where does it hurt?"

Eloise partially opened her eyes and wheezed, "What?" Her eyes shut and Rose heard her gasping for air.

"I don't like the look of her," Rose admitted. "I'd like to get her to hospital but Nanyuki is too far and I'm not sure they'll be any doctors on duty in Isiolo."

She sat on the edge of the bed and took hold of Eloise's arm. She said to Hellen, "I need to check her pulse. Can you time a minute for me?"

Hellen unbuckled her watch and held it before her.

"Whenever you're ready," said Rose.

"Now," replied Hellen.

The room was quiet. Eloise's breathing was coarse and rasping.

"Stop," called Hellen.

Rose bit her lip. Eloise's pulse was only fifty-six beats a minute. Too low. Her blood would not be able to reach the vital areas of her body, such as her brain. But what was causing her heart to slow?

She turned to Hellen. "This evening Eloise thought her cramps were caused by something she ate at supper. But food poisoning wouldn't be slowing her heart rate. There must be another explanation. Has she taken any medication? Any sleeping pills or anti-depressants?"

"I don't know." Hellen stood so she could open the drawer in the bedside table. It was empty. "I'll check in the bathroom." She returned with a small bottle, which she handed to Rose.

"Sorry, I can't read it without my glasses." Rose gave the bottle back. "What does it say?"

Hellen read, "Ambien. Underneath something beginning with Z and Tartrate." Hellen's hands trembled as she held the bottle.

"What about the back?" asked Rose. "Are there any words you recognise?"

"Benzodiazepine." Hellen looked enquiringly at Rose.

Rose tapped her leg. "An overdose of that would cause abdominal pains, lethargy and breathing irregularities. But I'm not sure about the low pulse. Could she have taken an overdose?"

Hellen emptied the contents of the white plastic container into an empty glass. "How many pills is an overdose? There are a lot left in this bottle."

Rose bit her lip. "I doubt it's those then, unless she had another bottle."

Hellen pinched her lips together and shook her head. "I didn't find one. And I checked the dustbin. But why would she take an overdose?"

Hellen returned the pills to the bottle and screwed on the cap.

Rose sighed. "I've no idea. Although her sister's death clearly upset her. Have you been with her all evening?"

"Mostly. I've kept popping back to our room next door, to check that the children are OK, and I went to speak to Alex in the bar, and buy some water. But I was only away ten minutes, if that." Hellen wrung her hands.

"I don't really understand," said Rose. "Maybe something else made her ill. Perhaps she took some pills, believing they would help her sleep."

Rose was thinking out loud. "And she reacted badly to them." She paused. "Or maybe she's taking some other medication and the two don't mix." Rose smoothed a strand of hair away from Eloise's face. She was very still.

Rose made up her mind. "She needs to go to hospital."

"But how?" asked Hellen. "I'm too scared to drive on these roads at night, especially with the bandits around Archer's Post, and Guy and Alex have been drinking all evening."

Rose turned to Eloise and shook her gently. "Eloise."

There was no response.

"Eloise, can you hear me?"

Hellen gasped.

"She's not dead," said Rose. "Not yet, but she is unconscious." Rose felt helpless. Useless. All she could do was watch Eloise die. But unless she knew what was making her ill, she couldn't cure her.

Hellen held Eloise's limp hand. She looked up sharply at Rose. "I can't feel anything."

Rose took Eloise's wrist. "There's still a pulse but it's very weak. We're losing her. I'd better fetch her husband."

Rose stood, but Hellen grabbed her arm.

"No! Stay with me. With Eloise. There's nothing Guy can do for her now."

Rose sat on the bed feeling utterly dejected as she watched, helpless to prevent a second young woman die in a week.

CHAPTER THIRTY-FOUR

Rose heard knocking and someone called, "Rose, are you awake?"

Her heartbeat raced as she jumped out of bed and flung the door open, "What's happened? Is someone else ill?"

Chloe stepped back into the corridor. "I've no idea. Why should anyone be ill?"

Rose leaned against the doorjamb and waited for her pulse to slow.

Chloe moved forward and touched her shoulder. "Are you OK? Has something happened?"

"Yes," Rose whispered, still catching her breath. "Eloise Ramsey died in the night. And I was with her."

Chloe gasped and covered her mouth with her hand. "No, I don't believe you. There was nothing wrong with her yesterday."

"Apart from her stomach cramps in the evening."

Chloe's voice was shaky as she said, "But surely they were from something she ate, which upset her tummy."

"That's what I thought, but it turned out to be far more serious." Rose realised that Chloe was dressed in her gloves and jacket, and she remembered the Great Grevy's Rally. She asked, "Are you ready to leave for today's census session?"

"Yes, that's why I came to get you."

Rose stood up and replied, "I don't think I should go. I'm shattered and I might need to speak to the police. But let me throw on some clothes and I'll join you outside."

Once again Rose hastily pulled on her trousers, jacket and shoes and rushed outside. She spotted the large figure of Sam. He was leaning forward and talking earnestly with Gabriel and Alex Newton.

Tessa rushed past Rose and joined her brother. Rose noted that Tessa's self-assured manner was lacking as she stood with her hands in her pockets, and her head and shoulders bowed forward.

As Rose approached, she heard Alex address his sister. "I was just telling Gabriel that we won't be able to undertake our census work today. Not after last night's tragedy."

"But I still want to go," insisted Tessa. "I can't hang around here all day doing nothing."

"But you can't go on your own," pleaded Alex.

"No, you can't," confirmed Sam. He looked over Tessa's shoulder at Rose and then strode across to meet her. He lowered his voice and said, "Are you OK? You look as if you've just woken up."

"I have. I was awake most of last night attending to Eloise Ramsey."

"Oh, I see," Sam nodded his head. "Then I think you should stay at the lodge. It's going to be another long, hot day. Besides, I've just had a message from Judy to say that she's on her way. Apparently Ms Rotich is insisting that the Nanyuki authorities are involved in Eloise Ramsey's death, because it comes so soon after her sister's."

"Well, she has a point," conceded Rose.

"Sam," Gabriel called.

"Do you mind?" Sam asked.

"No, you go and help sort things out."

Rose joined Chloe and Pearl. Chloe was sitting in the driver's seat of her Land Cruiser, facing out, with the door open. Pearl leaned against the side of the car.

"What a terrible business," said Chloe, drawing her knees up and clutching her legs.

Pearl remarked, "Don't you find it strange? That group pretend to be friends but they're always sniping at each other."

Sam approached them and Tessa followed him, but hung back, her arms by her side.

Sam said, "If it's OK with you, Tessa will take Mama Rose's place. And we'll split her team's census area between ourselves and another group."

Pearl walked over to Tessa and introduced herself. "Welcome to the team. I'm Pearl and Chloe is driving. I guess you've already met Sam."

Tessa kept her head bowed as her eyes rose to meet Pearl's. "Thank you. Though I doubt I'll be much use today."

Rose indicated to Sam, and they stepped away from Chloe's car.

She said, "I'm not sure what the relationship was between Tessa Newton and the deceased. I understand that Eloise financed Guy, her husband, to buy into the Newtons' safari business.

"And he became a partner alongside Tessa's brother Alex. But I understand the business is in trouble and Eloise may have been considering a further investment or even a buyout. Tessa is very protective about the company and I think she believes it should have been left to her and not her brother."

Sam pulled at his chin. "So you think Tessa had a reason for wanting Eloise dead?"

"I'm not sure I would go as far as that, not yet anyway. But it might be worth probing Tessa to see if you can discover her side of the story."

Sam looked across at Tessa and replied, "I can try, but she doesn't look particularly responsive today."

CHAPTER THIRTY-FIVE

Rose waved Chloe and her team off and returned to her room. She contemplated returning to bed but doubted she would sleep, so instead she took a shower.

She packed a book and her glasses into her green tote bag and headed to the restaurant for breakfast. It was deserted and as she looked around, she felt an emptiness inside her.

A waiter asked, "Table for one?"

She turned to him and asked, "Can I take something out to the viewing platform by the pool?"

"Of course, memsahib."

She filled a bowl with fruit and picked up a pot of strawberry yoghurt."

"What would you like to drink?" The waiter asked, placing her bowl and yoghurt on a tray and adding a napkin and cutlery.

"Kericho Gold tea, please."

She wandered through the deserted hotel to the outdoor viewing area. The sun had risen and as she sat down she was comforted by its first warming rays.

She ate her breakfast in silence, watching the baboons from the previous evening clamber down from the doum palm and begin their daily activities. The adults sat around in a circle, grooming and picking ticks and other insects from each other's fur.

On the far riverbank, two giraffes wandered to the water's edge. They spread their front legs as they bent their long necks down to drink.

Rose pulled on her wide-brimmed sun hat and opened her book. She could hear the chirping of birds, and the occasional call or snort of an animal, and she felt more at peace with herself.

She'd slept fitfully and had woken several times. She'd been wracked with guilt about Eloise's death and her inability to prevent it. But she was not a doctor, nor had she any idea what had made Eloise ill.

And then there was Rebecca's death less than a week ago. She also had no idea what had caused that. Were the two linked? How could they be? And yet, the mere fact that both deaths were unexplained was suspicious.

She knew she shouldn't get involved. Craig would have told her to leave the matter with the police, especially as Constable Wachira was on her way to interview Eloise's husband and friends about her death.

There had been another disturbing element to her dreams, and once again she felt drawn back to fleeting, and disturbing, memories from her childhood. But nothing took shape, and she had no idea what it all meant.

She looked over her book, which she hadn't started reading, at the young baboons as they raced about, chasing each other and rolling in the dust. A large male strutted about on all fours displaying his prominent red, furless bottom. He sat down and scratched his neck.

Rose felt an itch on her shoulder and stretched across with her arm but couldn't reach it. The sisters' deaths were like an itch which she couldn't scratch and, until she could, and their deaths had been explained, she knew they would continue to bother her.

Five minutes later the peace was broken as she heard Alex Newton announce, "Let's grab a coffee. The sun's shining on the viewing platform, and you can't mope around in your room all morning waiting for the police to arrive."

The waiter removed Rose's breakfast items. She asked, "Can I have another cup of tea?"

He nodded and approached Alex and Guy who had taken a table at the edge of the viewing platform. Alex said, "A cappuccino and a black coffee, please."

"And a brandy," Guy added in a resigned tone.

"Do you think that's wise? It could be a long day with the police."

"Exactly," quipped Guy.

Rose watched them over the top of her book. Guy leaned forward and placed his arms and his head on the table.

Rose tried to concentrate on her book, but after only a minute she heard Guy mutter, "I don't understand why Hellen didn't fetch me. She didn't give me a chance to say goodbye."

"Please don't have a go at Hellen. She did her best and was the only one who actually helped Eloise. Her and the old lady."

Rose raised her book to hide her face from the two men.

Alex continued, "Besides, she came to the bar and told us Eloise was feeling unwell."

"Yes, but she said it was just stomach cramps. I didn't think it was anything to worry about."

"None of us did," consoled Alex.

"I know Hellen thinks I didn't care for Eloise. And like most people, she believes I was only after her money. And I admit, that's how it started. Granny Edna was always so bitter and forbid me to have anything to do with the Munros, because they stole our family's land. But I really did love her. More than I realised. And now I can never tell her."

There was laughter and rushing feet as Alex's daughter ran out onto the viewing platform and threw herself at her father.

"Daddy, are you coming swimming?" Mia asked excitedly.

"Not yet, sweetheart."

Hellen followed, supporting Liam on her hip and carrying a large, striped bag. Her cheeks and eyes were sunken into her face and her voice was hollow as she said, "Come with me, Mia. Leave Daddy to talk to Uncle Guy."

She put her bag on the table closest to the pool and removed a flotation vest. She placed Liam on the ground and zipped Mia into the vest.

Liam crawled along the decking. Hellen jumped up and grabbed him before he toppled over the edge.

The waiter arrived with Rose's tea. He leaned towards Rose and whispered, "Sergeant

Muthoni and Constable Wachira have arrived and are asking for you."

Rose looked down at her tea cup and jug of hot water and said, "I guess I'll have to save these for later."

She walked into the reception area and was greeted by Constable Wachira.

"Habari, Mama Rose. This is Sergeant Muthoni from Isiolo police station. Technically, this is his case."

Sergeant Muthoni was a genial looking man with curly grey hair. He said, "You're welcome to it. You and that Ms Rotich. I'll speak to the lodge staff and you can interview the witnesses and next of kin."

Sergeant Muthoni walked around the reception desk and disappeared through an open door behind it.

"It looks like it's just the two of us," Constable Wachira commented. "And I understand Sam is out undertaking the Grevy's census."

"He's with Chloe and Pearl, and one of the dead woman's associates, Tessa Newton. Tessa insisted on joining the census today, rather than staying here, but she looked rather distraught. Sam's going to see if he can find out anything from her that's relevant to the dead woman, and her death."

Constable Wachira nodded.

"OK. The body has been removed and is being taken to the Cottage Hospital so perhaps you could walk me through yesterday evening's events."

CHAPTER THIRTY-SIX

The sun was as relentless in Samburu National Reserve as it had been the previous day. Pearl rested the large camera on her lap as she stared out of the car window at the parched landscape.

Apart from day trips to Nairobi National Park, and the odd excursions to Tsavo or Nakuru National Parks, she had not been on many safaris.

Chloe interrupted her thoughts and asked, "Pearl, what are you thinking about? You look miles away."

"I was thinking how different Samburu is from Nairobi National Park. I was conscious of the change in landscape after we passed through Isiolo, as the only things which seemed to be growing were thorn trees. And the people appear much poorer, living in simple huts with grass and plastic-covered roofs, and a few skinny sheep and goats wandering about."

Sam remarked, "It's a different way of life than we're used to. Most of these people still adhere to their tribal customs and way of life. And whilst they may appear to live in poverty, for many their daily requirements are much simpler."

"This is the furthest north I've ventured. What's it like beyond here, towards Lake Turkana?" asked Pearl.

"Hot and dry," declared Sam. "And I wouldn't recommend driving unless you're with someone who knows the area. The towns are fewer and the distance between them greater, and groups of bandits roam the area and prey on travellers."

"I'd like to visit Lake Turkana," revealed Chloe. "But I think I'd prefer to fly. It must take an age to drive there."

Beside her, Pearl felt Tessa stir.

Tessa said in a quiet, wistful voice, "There's a wonderful, eco-friendly camp, Desert Rose, which is south of Lake Turkana. I've stayed there with clients and, as it's built in a cedar forest, the surrounding area is very green. But you can take day excursions or overnight camping trips to Lake Turkana. I particularly enjoy boat safaris on the lake."

Pearl turned to Tessa and asked, "Do you enjoy your job?"

"I love visiting different places. But I think I'm getting too old, and I certainly have less patience to deal with large groups of tourists who only want to follow the standard itineraries. I much prefer escorting smaller parties to remote areas, but my opportunities are limited and my work is dictated by others.

"As I'm freelance, I have some choice about where I go, but not that much as I have to earn a living, and it's not getting any easier. The tour companies are starting to favour younger guides who have more energy and enthusiasm than me. What I really want is a chance to run my own tour company and target clients for specialist trips. But it's not easy breaking into that market without the backing of an established business."

In the front passenger seat Sam said, "Steady. I think there may be a Grevy's zebra hiding at the back of that small herd of Burchell's."

Chloe slowed down.

"That one, on the left. It looks larger than the others and has those large, round ears," observed Pearl.

"Yes, that's the one," agreed Sam. "But it will be difficult to photograph it without spooking the entire herd. Chloe can you drive around the back of group and we'll see if we can get close to the Grevy's."

Chloe turned off the track and they slowly bumped their way over the uneven ground as they skirted the zebra herd.

"Watch out for that termite mound," called Sam, touching the windscreen.

Pearl lowered her window and prepared the camera. The Grevy's zebra turned to watch them and she quickly took a burst of photos. Then the whole herd tossed their heads and trotted away.

"Did you get it?" asked Sam.

"I think so," Pearl replied.

As Chloe drove carefully back to the track Sam asked, "So what are you going to do with yourself, Pearl? Do you fancy becoming a safari tour guide?"

Pearl packed the camera back into its case. "Not likely. I prefer my home comforts. Besides, I don't have the patience to deal with endless stupid questions and requests."

"What about college?" Sam pressed.

"I thought I wanted to go but now I'm not sure. I'd still like to design clothes, but a small range for my own shop."

"Would you have them made in Kenya? Out of Kanga?" asked Sam.

Pearl mused, "I don't think so, other companies are already doing that. I visited a factory on my recent trip to India, and they'd be willing to produce a small line of clothing for me, using a soft-cotton material with a huge range of patterns."

Chloe manoeuvred around another termite mound. The lopsided tower of baked red earth stood at least a metre high.

Sam looked at her and asked, "And what about you. Are you going to look for a job in Nanyuki?"

Chloe tapped the steering wheel. "I'm not sure what I could do. Then there's the issue of obtaining a work permit, which I need even for voluntary work."

Pearl leaned forward between the front seats and suggested, "Why not join me in opening a shop. What about a range of European style clothing?"

Chloe turned left at junction and headed towards the river. "I worked in a clothing shop in London. It was very high end and great fun, but the clothes wouldn't be practical for Africa. And who would pay the exorbitant prices? Besides, I've no idea how to import them."

Pearl pressed, "But you did appear keen about the idea of opening a shop."

Chloe tilted her head to one side. "What I'd really like, is to be able to buy a range of good quality food items in Nanyuki. And grab a quick, tasty sandwich or salad. Eateries either close at two pm or the service is so slow I can't be bothered to wait."

Tessa nodded, "I know what you mean. I find myself grabbing a bag of chips or a couple of samosas when I'm busy."

"Exactly. The UK has wonderful local delis which double up as small cafes. That's the sort of place I'd love to run."

"So why don't you?" enquired Sam.

They reached a T-junction of tracks. "Which way?" asked Chloe.

"Turn right. We need to carry on into Tessa's team's census area," instructed Sam.

Chloe turned onto another track and said, "I guess I haven't thought about it that seriously. There would be a lot to do. As well as sourcing stock, and transporting it to Nanyuki, there's all the bureaucracy and paperwork involved with obtaining a work permit."

"There is, but it's far easier if you're self-employed and giving jobs to Kenyan's, rather

248

than being employed, where you are viewed as taking a job opportunity away from a Kenyan."

Chloe pressed the accelerator as they skidded over sandy ground. "And then the premises would have to be right. Somewhere bright and airy, with plenty of room, and outside space for tables and chairs. I've not seen anything like that in Nanyuki."

Tessa suggested, "You should speak to my sister-in-law, Hellen, and see if she can find you suitable premises. She's working really hard at the moment, but I don't think she's actually sold or let any properties. And I know she's desperate for the money."

"Did you see her this morning?" asked Sam.

"Briefly. All the early morning activity woke the children, but she looked exhausted. I think Liam kept her awake during the night, and she was pretty distraught about Eloise's death." Tessa turned and looked out of the car window.

"How do you feel about it?" Sam probed.

"Nothing," replied Tessa. "I just feel numb."

Pearl turned to Tessa and asked, "Were you good friends?"

"Not really. She and Guy were friends with Alex and Hellen, and I only saw her with them."

Sam turned around and said, "And what about the safari business, was she involved with that?"

"I've no idea," Tessa replied sharply, and turned to look out of the window.

CHAPTER THIRTY-SEVEN

After Rose had finished explaining the previous evening's events, and Constable Wachira had examined Eloise's room, they walked out onto the viewing platform by the swimming pool.

The waiter approached Rose and enquired, "Would you like your tea now?"

"Yes, please." Rose's mouth was dry.

"And for you?" he asked the constable.

"A Diet Coke, or a tea if you don't have one."

Alex Newton and Guy Ramsey were watching them.

Constable Wachira said, "I'd better speak to Hellen Newton first, as she was with you when Mrs Ramsey died."

Rose sat down.

Constable Wachira walked across to Hellen, who was trying to entertain her son with toy cars and supervise her daughter, who was splashing around in the shallow end of the pool.

Constable Wachira bent down to speak to Hellen, who then stood up, looked across at her husband and called, "Alex, can you look after the children whilst I speak to the police?"

"Of course, darling." Alex took Liam from his mother and walked across to the swimming pool.

"Look at me, Daddy," cried his daughter and she ducked her head under the water.

Constable Wachira and Hellen joined Rose.

Rose noted that Hellen's eyes were bloodshot. She asked kindly, "Did you get much sleep last night?"

"No, I was too upset and then Liam kept waking up crying. He's teething you see."

"What can you tell me about last night?" Constable Wachira asked.

Hellen Newton ran through the events.

Rose half-listened to Hellen's account as she watched Guy, who was now sitting on his own. He hadn't shaved and his linen shirt was creased and the buttons didn't align. He gazed out at the river.

Fergus Peacock strode over to join him. He looked down at Guy and called towards a waiter, "Two whiskeys please." He sat down and said, "You look terrible. One might even think you loved your wife."

"Shut up, Fergus," Guy spat. "What are you doing here anyway?"

"Now you're the sole heir to the Munro fortune, we need to make plans. You remember what we discussed last week?"

Fergus leaned closer to Guy, and Rose was unable to catch what he said.

Guy sat back and stated, "Not now, not today."

The waiter returned with their whiskies, and Guy downed his.

Constable Wachira finished her questions and said, "Thank you, Mrs Newton."

Hellen joined her husband by the pool as Constable Wachira approached Guy and Fergus. She said, "Mr Ramsey, can I speak to you now?"

"I'll be off then," said Fergus, lifting his glass.

"And you are?" asked the young constable.

"Fergus Peacock."

"And were you with the party yesterday?"

"Only for part of it," Fergus tipped back his glass.

Guy looked at him coldly and said, "As you were with us on the Grevy's Rally, and in the evening for supper, I'd say that was a substantial part of the day."

Constable Wachira crossed her arms and said, "So would I. Please stay here and I will speak to you next. Mr Ramsey," she indicated for Guy to join her at Rose's table.

When they were seated, Constable Wachira divulged, "We found some sleeping tablets in your wife's room."

"She was prescribed those last week, as she was struggling to sleep after Becky's death."

"Was she depressed? Could she have taken an overdose?" Constable Wachira pressed.

Guy rubbed his eye. "She was upset, and at times distraught, and blamed herself for Becky's death. But there's no way she would have killed herself."

Rose leaned forward and asked, "Why did she blame herself for her sister's death."

"Because she had insisted Becky return to Kenya and help sort out their parents' estate. If she hadn't, she said Becky would still be alive."

Rose probed, "Did your wife inherit her sister's part of the estate?"

Guy licked his lips, "Yes."

"But Becky was due to get married. Was she changing her will?" asked Rose.

Guy's lips trembled. "I've no idea. You'll have to speak to her lawyer."

"Would that be Fergus Peacock?" enquired Constable Wachira.

"He's dealing with the Kenyan side of things. But I believe she also had a UK lawyer. You'll have to ask Fergus."

Rose sat back, considering what Guy had told them.

Constable Wachira continued interviewing Guy.

Rose watched Fergus who stood and joined Hellen, who had returned to her table with Liam. Fergus bowed his head and said something to Hellen that Rose could not catch, but she saw his predatory expression.

Alex carried Mia across to the table wrapped in a towel. He looked at Hellen's face, turned to Fergus and said, "I think that's quite enough. There's no need to keep upsetting Hellen. She's told you she'll get the money, and we shall."

Constable Wachira finished questioning Guy. He stood up and walked across to Alex and buried his head in Alex's shoulder. Alex stood frozen as Guy's body began to shake. Hellen stood up and guided Guy to a chair and wrapped her arms around him.

Constable Wachira called, "Mr Peacock. Can we speak to you now?"

Fergus Peacock sat down, stretched out his legs and crossed his ankles.

"I understand you were a friend of Mrs Ramsey's, as well as her lawyer."

"That is correct." He looked politely at the young constable.

Mia, who was now wearing a floral dress, rolled a small bottle, with a black top, along the viewing deck.

"And you were with her yesterday for the first day of the Great Grevy's Rally."

"Again, that is correct." Fergus shuffled in his seat.

"And did you notice anything untoward?"

"What do you mean by that?" Fergus looked over at the young girl and then Alex and Guy. He appeared flustered.

Constable Wachira continued, "Did you notice anything which disturbed Mrs Ramsey?"

Alex walked across to Mia and handed her one of Liam's toy cars. "Here play with this." He picked up the bottle and placed it on a table.

Fergus's attention returned to Constable Wachira, and he said, "I think her sister's death was still playing on her mind. She'd been very upset all week, and often broke down in tears."

A waiter removed the bottle and approached Alex, Guy and Hellen.

"And when did you first notice that she was ill?"

"She started complaining of stomach cramps during supper. Hellen took her back to her room and that's the last I saw of her. I'm not staying at this lodge."

"And you didn't notice anything else?"

"Not that comes to mind. Tessa seemed rather short with Eloise so I'm not sure if they'd fallen out. Not that they were the best of friends anyway."

The waiter took orders from Alex and Hellen, and returned to the bar at the rear of the viewing platform.

Constable Wachira continued, "I understand Guy Ramsey is the sole beneficiary of his wife's estate. Is that a substantial amount?"

Fergus leaned back and laced his fingers together. "It will be when the court confirms the application to declare Eloise's parents dead. And we expect a decision shortly."

"And Mrs Ramsey's sister, Rebecca. Does her estate now pass to Mr Ramsey?"

"It does." Fergus tapped the ends of his fingers together.

"But was she making a new will in favour of her fiancé?"

"I'm not at liberty to say." Fergus's expression was blank.

"But you can provide us with details of Miss Munro's British lawyer."

"I should be able to. They will be at my office in Nairobi."

He examined his hands.

"Thank you, Mr Peacock. I'll be in touch if I have any further questions."

Constable Wachira then interviewed Alex Newton, but Rose didn't learn anything new.

Finally, the constable turned to her and said, "Shall we see if Sergeant Muthoni has anything to report?"

As they passed the bar, Rose noticed the small bottle with the black lid. She picked it up and handed it to Constable Wachira. "Can your lab discover what was in this bottle?"

"Why?"

"I don't know, but I have a feeling it's significant."

CHAPTER THIRTY-EIGHT

Sunday night at Punda Milia Lodge was subdued. Sam and many of those involved with the Great Grevy's Rally had already left. Rose, Chloe and Pearl kept the topics of conversation upbeat over supper and retired to their rooms early.

On Monday morning, Chloe pulled to a stop outside Rose's house and said in an apologetic tone, "I'm sorry the weekend wasn't as much fun as we'd hoped. Will you be OK?"

There was a scraping noise as Samwell opened the front gate without securing one of the metal bolts, so that it dragged along the ground.

"Yes, although I'll miss Kipto as she's on leave until tomorrow."

Samwell picked up Rose's bag, and she followed him around to the front of the house. He stopped before he reached the patio doors and looked back at her uncertainly.

"What's the matter?" She asked, and joining Samwell, she noticed broken glass on the painted concrete floor.

"Wait here, Mama," said Samwell, as he pushed open the door and stepped inside the living room.

While Rose waited for him to reappear, she called Constable Wachira.

"Mama Rose, I don't have any news for you yet on Eloise Ramsey's autopsy, or the contents of the bottle you gave me."

"I'm afraid that's not the reason I'm calling. You see someone has broken into my house."

Constable Wachira groaned. "I'll come straight over. Is there much damage?"

"I'm not sure. Samwell is checking inside at the moment. I hope the culprits aren't still here."

As Rose finished her call, Samwell reappeared shaking his head. "Nobody here. But Kipto be cross about mess."

Rose stepped over the glass into the living room. Her eyes were drawn to the bookshelf and trophy display cabinet on the far wall, by the fireplace. There were a number of gaps where books had been removed and many of the trophies were missing, including a large gold tankard with a lid, which she'd been considering donating to the polo club as Craig's memorial trophy.

She uncharacteristically swore under her breath.

She observed the white patches on the walls where paintings of dogs, cows and horses had been removed before walking across to a side table. It had displayed a small collection of silver boxes, some glass ornaments and two porcelain figurines. They were all gone.

A silver framed photograph lay face down and she turned it over with relief. Although the glass was smashed, the photograph of herself and Craig, with their children Chris and Heather, at the beach twenty-five years ago was still intact.

"Habari," called Constable Wachira.

"I'm inside. Be careful, there's broken glass by the door," Rose replied.

"That'll be how they got in then." Constable Wachira stepped inside and gazed around. "Oh dear. The thieves are getting bolder. And it looks like they've taken their time. Am I correct in thinking there's quite a lot missing?"

Rose nodded glumly. "I've no idea if the items they stole had any real value, but each meant something to me."

Constable Wachira walked across to the far side of the room, picked up a book about Kikuyu history off the floor, and placed it back in the bookshelf.

"Oh no," cried Rose. "They've taken Craig's bird book."

"What a mess," said Pearl appearing in the doorway. "Thanks for your call, Judy. I'm afraid Thabiti's out, but what can I do to help?"

"We need to make an inventory of all the missing items."

"Don't worry about cleaning up," said Rose. "Kipto will sort everything out when she returns. We'll only irritate her if we put things back in the wrong place."

Rose slumped down on the edge of the sofa. She couldn't face looking in any of the other rooms.

Pearl walked across to the bedroom door and asked, "Shall I check what damage has been done through here?"

"Thank you," Rose responded gratefully. "And can you also check Craig's office, which is through the door at the far end?"

Constable Wachira followed Pearl but soon returned. "There's far less mess through there, and it doesn't look as if much has been taken. Will you be all right sleeping here on your own tonight?"

Pearl returned and suggested, "Would you like to stay at Guinea Fowl Cottage? You know you're welcome at any time."

Rose felt violated. Someone she didn't know had invaded her space, touching and messing with her belongings. The items weren't just objects, but memories, and she felt as if the thieves had trampled through her life.

She looked up at Pearl. "Thank you, but I want to stay here, close to my things. But I'll stay in the guest cottage and ask Samwell if he'll sleep in the house tonight."

CHAPTER THIRTY-NINE

Rose decided she needed to keep herself busy on Tuesday morning and with an activity which was outside, and away from her house. She had received an email from the father of a young polo player, who was building stables on land he had bought near Timau. His daughter had asked for samples of her digestive and calming herbal mixes.

She stood in a lean-to wooden shed beside open sacks of dried herbs. Although the recipes for the mixtures were pinned to the wall, she knew the required proportions off-by-heart. She scooped dried chamomile leaves into a large bucket, as they were the key ingredient for her calming mix.

Samwell poked his head into the shed and informed her, "The Commissioner and young police woman are here to see you."

"Thank you," replied Rose, wiping her hands on her trousers.

She walked around the side of the house, avoiding the kitchen and living room, but there was no sign of the police officers. She heard voices from inside the living room.

Commissioner Akida pulled open the patio doors and stepped over the broken glass.

He saw Rose and said, "Pole, Mama. The thieves have made quite a mess. I'd like to make these burglaries a priority, but Ms Rotich is insistent we gather more evidence about the sisters' deaths for her inquest. I am not sure if she believes the deaths are linked, or whether they just provide her with further press opportunities.

"Either way, our new coroner is no longer content with phoning me but barges into my office several times a day demanding updates.

Of course, she doesn't have to actually prove anything. Apparently that is my job and as far as I'm concerned we have two regrettable, but unrelated deaths. There is no evidence that the women died from anything other than natural causes. It's such a circus. I can no longer think straight."

The Commissioner removed his cap and scratched his head.

Rose shuffled backwards in surprise. She'd rarely heard the commissioner make such a long or impassioned speech. "I'm sorry the new coroner is upsetting the status quo. And Rebecca and Eloise's deaths are a conundrum. Have you had the results of Eloise's autopsy?"

Constable Wachira stepped out from behind the commissioner and replied, "It's the same as it was for her sister, Miss Munro. Mrs Ramsey was fit and healthy and the pathologist could find no reason for her death."

Rose pulled out a chair and indicated for the others to sit down at the outdoor dining table.

The constable placed her notebook and pen on the table and reported, "But the pathologist was intrigued by the contents of your bottle. They were plant based and he's sent them to Nairobi for further analysis, along with blood samples from each of the dead women."

There was a patter of small feet and Thabiti's fluffy white dog raced around the corner. She placed her front paws on the commissioner's legs and yapped expectantly.

"Down Pixel," said Thabiti, but he picked her up as she ignored him.

Thabiti looked around. "Where are Potto and Izzy?"

Rose replied, "They've been hiding since the break-in. Potto's in the staff quarters, being fed titbits I suspect, and Izzy's still lying on the bed in the guest cottage where I slept."

"Were you OK there?" Thabiti asked, sitting between Rose and Constable Wachira. "Pearl said she invited you to stay at ours and the offer's still open."

Rose placed her hand on his arm. "Thank you. But now I've survived the first night I think I'll be OK. Besides, I want to spend as much time as I can here before I have to move."

"Move?" asked the commissioner, his voice rising in pitch.

"Yes, I'm afraid so. The landlord is selling this plot. Hellen Newton has persuaded him to give me a month's extension but I have to leave by the end of August, and find somewhere else for my animals, staff and myself to live." Rose rubbed her forehead and said, "And I suppose I'd better start looking, and asking around."

"But you will stay in Nanyuki?" the commissioner pressed.

"I'm not sure. The rents are high and still rising. I may have to look closer to Timau, especially if I want a house with land for my animals."

Thabiti put Pixel down and she scampered into the garden. He looked towards the patio doors and said, "I came to see if I can help tidy up?"

"Thank you. Kipto will see to most of it but perhaps you could look at Craig's office. I've not had the energy to venture in there yet."

The commissioner turned to Thabiti. "Were you on the expedition searching for missing aeroplanes? The one which has caused our new coroner such excitement?"

"I did venture up the Aberdares with Pete Stephenson on Friday. But why is the coroner interested in our discoveries? One was the wreckage of a World War II bomber and the other was the Munros' light aircraft, which is surely the jurisdiction of either Naivasha or Nyahururu?"

The commissioner pulled at his collar. "You would think so, but no. Ms Rotich has decided the plane crash and the deaths of Rebecca Munro and Eloise Ramsey are linked, despite being nine years apart."

"Why?" asked Thabiti. Pixel returned from the garden, sniffed around the patio and with her nose to the ground set off towards the nearest guest cottage.

Constable Wachira half raised her hand, and said, "Sir, if I may."

"Go ahead, Constable."

"If Ms Rotich is involved, it means she has something to gain either financially or politically."

"Most astute, Constable. So what do you surmise in this case?"

"I suspect both, sir. The discovery of the plane, and confirmation of the deaths of two wealthy Kenyans, combined with the recent and unexplained deaths of their daughters, will soon catch the press's imagination. No doubt she will want to take the credit for resolving their deaths."

"Quite so," the commissioner nodded glumly.

"And she may scent money, as there could be considerable death duties to pay."

The commissioner leaned back. "That wasn't something I had considered, but you're quite right."

Rose said, "I believe Rebecca Munro was in Kenya to sort out her parents' estate. And that an application had been made to court to declare them legally dead."

Thabiti added, "But as long as the skeletons found in the plane are those of the Munros then that step can now be bypassed. Were they very wealthy?"

Constable Wachira twirled her pen. "Apparently, although I understand they set up tax efficient vehicles, such as trusts for their daughters. That's what they've both been living on."

Rose added, "I've heard that part of Eloise's trust was invested, by her husband, in the Newtons' safari business."

"Is that so?" said the commissioner. "I've seen a copy of the parents' will, and it leaves everything to their daughters, apart from a few gifts they made to their staff. The girls honoured those after their parents' disappearance."

Constable Wachira referred to her notebook, "Mr Peacock, the family lawyer, confirmed that Rebecca Munro's estate passed to Eloise on her death, and from Eloise to her husband, Guy Ramsey. He inherits it all. But it might have been different if Miss Munro had died after her marriage. I'm still waiting for Mr Peacock to provide details of Miss Munro's UK lawyer."

Commissioner Akida leaned back. "I wonder if Ms Rotich does think she can get her hands on any of the money."

Rose mused, "And I wonder what cut the family lawyer is taking?"

CHAPTER FORTY

R ose, Thabiti, Commissioner Akida and Constable Wachira sat in thoughtful silence at the old dining table on Rose's patio. Kipto appeared around the corner of the cottage carrying a battered suitcase, tied shut with string. She dumped it on the ground and cried, "Mama, what happen? Samwell said house a mess and thieves take many things."

"He's right. You better look for yourself," Rose replied dully.

Kipto's shoes scrunched the broken glass as she opened the patio door and peered in side. Her hand shot to her mouth as she gasped. She turned, shaking her head and said, "Bad men."

Looking around the group at the table, she announced, "Good, you find them. And I make tea and coffee."

Pixel raced onto the patio and followed Kipto, who lifted her suitcase and bustled into the house.

Thabiti commented, "I think she believes we're here to solve Mama Rose's break-in."

"And I will do," bridled Constable Wachira.

Rose leaned back and gazed out into the garden. "Of course. There's not just money at stake in respect of the Munro family. There's also property, principally a house and land at Nyeri, whose ownership I believe is disputed, although not necessarily in the legal sense."

"What do you mean?" asked the commissioner.

"I've heard mention of Guy Ramsey's grandmother, Edna. She's an artist who lives in Nairobi, and it seems that she raised Guy. But she was very bitter towards the Munro family who she believes stole her family's land." Rose pinched her lips and added, "I wonder if that land is a place called Roho House, at Nyeri."

Thabiti raised his head sharply. "Otto mentioned Roho House as we drove to the Aberdares to start our plane expedition. He was searching for, and discovered, the Munro's light aircraft."

"Who is Otto?" asked the commissioner. "I recognise the name."

"A young mzungu with very fair curly hair, which tends to flop over his face," replied Rose. "I think he and Rebecca Munro were childhood friends."

Thabiti's eyes shone. "That's right. He told me he spent time with her family at Roho House when they were kids. And that his father was the manager of the neighbouring tea estate, which the Munros and Ramseys used to own."

"That backs up Edna's story about land, although I'm not sure if she was referring to Roho House or the tea plantation," mused Rose.

"There are plenty of tea plantations in Nyeri," stated the commissioner.

"It's the perfect location with its rich volcanic soil, plentiful rain and a high altitude, which combines sunshine with cooler air. The British colonial authorities saw it as the perfect cash crop to help pay for administering the East African Protectorate, as Kenya was known at the turn of the twentieth century. A significant amount of Kikuyu tribal land around Nyeri was redistributed to European settlers."

"I drove past the very neat and tidy Kenya Chai Producers' estate, on the way into Nyeri," said Thabiti, "and I stopped next to it searching for the proposed new brewery site."

The commissioner fiddled with his cap. "I hear its running into the same issues that a similar scheme did ten years ago."

Thabiti wrinkled his brow. "Do you mean the curse?"

The commissioner looked solemn. "Part of the site is held sacred by the Kikuyu. It's probably an ancient burial ground. So the Kikuyu elders placed a curse on anyone who disturbs the land."

Someone had also mentioned a curse to Rose at the Women's League meeting. "But Dora told me the land at Roho House is cursed."

Thabiti sat back. "When I stopped to look for the new brewery site, I parked by the entrance to a property which had a large house in the distance. An elderly Kikuyu man approached me and confirmed that the land behind the house was the site of the new brewery, and it was accessed through the property. And he also mentioned a curse. So I guess I was looking at Roho House, which belonged to the sisters, Rebecca and Eloise."

"It might well have been," agreed the commissioner, "but I'm not sure this has any bearing on the sisters' deaths."

Rose stood and walked across to the stone bird table. She began to break up a piece of stale bread she had left on it.

"So we have the Munro family, who supposedly cheated the Ramsey family out of land at Nyeri. Geraldine and Michael Munro decided to live in Nyeri, at Roho House, and raise a family. Then an international company wanted to develop a plot but they needed access through the Munros' property. They may even have offered to buy it.

"But the scheme never goes ahead and Michael and Geraldine disappear, and are presumed dead. Was it an accident or something more sinister? Whichever, it was enough to feed the story of the curse."

Thabiti jumped in. "And now Tucan Breweries is proposing to develop the sacred site again, and the owners of the access land inexplicably die. So the curse is responsible."

The commissioner sat up, "Am I really going back to Ms Rotich to tell her we've solved the riddle of the sisters' deaths and that they, and their parents, were killed by a Kikuyu curse?"

"She might find it hard to refute," stated Constable Wachira in a level tone. "If she denies that curses can cause deaths, she risks alienating a good proportion of the Kikuyu community."

"I think I'll save it as a last resort." The commissioner looked down at the table.

Constable Wachira tapped her pen against her notebook and looked across at Thabiti. "There was a young man who fits Otto's description at the Bushman's Restaurant, and he was seen arguing with Rebecca. And I think Guy Ramsey mentioned seeing him, but he must have left before I could get his details."

Thabiti drew a circle on the table with his finger. Without looking up he said, "Otto told me that he left as soon as Becky collapsed. I think he's been trying to muster the courage to speak to her again. He said his last words to her were spoken in anger."

Rose walked back onto the patio and said, "I don't know about the argument at the Bushman's but I was at Dormans when Becky, Rebecca, asked him to stop pestering her. He seemed to believe Rebecca should return to Kenya to marry him and, when she refused, he said something along the lines that if he couldn't have her, then nobody else could."

The commissioner sat up. "That's the first real motive I've heard."

Thabiti continued to stare at the table, but he shook his head. "I don't believe Otto would hurt Becky, never mind kill her. He was really cut up about her death. Besides, he told me that when he was walking towards her at the restaurant, someone threw something and then she collapsed."

"Threw something?" repeated Constable Wachira in a sharp tone. "That's the first time anyone has mentioned that. I definitely need to interview this Otto. And I'll ask Sam if he saw anything as he was coming out of the restaurant."

"It's certainly a more tangible lead than a Kikuyu curse," said the commissioner as he swept his cap off the table and stood up.

CHAPTER FORTY-ONE

T habiti left Mama Rose, Commissioner Akida and Constable Wachira on the patio and entered the house. Kipto had dropped her suitcase inside the door and draped her coat over the back of a chair. She must have forgotten about the hot drinks. Instead, she was tutting away in the corner of the room, picking up books and returning them to the bookcase.

She turned, holding up the pages of a book in one hand and the faded hardback cover in another. "Look at damage thieves cause. No respect for old things." She carefully placed the pages back in the cover and returned the book to its rightful place.

Thabiti searched the books and his heart sank. Craig's favourite bird book was missing. He left Kipto and walked quickly through Rose's bedroom, feeling the blood rise in his cheeks, and opened the door at the far end. He stepped into Craig's office and sighed with relief. It looked as if the thieves had only made a cursory search of this room.

He leaned down and picked a file up from the floor, and placed it back on the shelf. On the desk he rearranged papers, which were spread about, but stopped when he noticed a bill from the district hospital. It was for a total of fifty thousand shillings for Craig's cremation.

Behind it was another bill, for thirty-three thousand shillings, from Cape Chestnut for the wake, and there was a third invoice from the Cottage Hospital for a hundred and fifty thousand shillings. They all appeared to be outstanding, and now Mama Rose didn't even have the option of selling anything to settle them.

His phoned pinged. The message was from Pearl inviting him to join her and Chloe for lunch at Dormans. He better find Pixel and drop her back at Guinea Fowl Cottage.

Thabiti walked through the metal arch into the Dormans complex. Chloe and Pearl were seated at the round picnic-style table, on the right-hand side of the entrance.

Chloe beckoned to him. "How's Rose?"

"I'd say she's avoiding the fact that someone's broken into her cottage and stolen from her." Thabiti thought back to the unpaid bills which Rose also appeared to be ignoring.

Chloe picked up her teaspoon and tapped her cup. "It's terrible how people presume they can rummage through other people's belongings and take whatever they fancy. I've a hospital appointment on Thursday in Nairobi and I'm not sure I should go now, and leave the house empty."

Pearl looked at her and smiled, "Don't worry. I'll house-sit for you."

Chloe gasped, "You can't do that. What if the thieves come, find you there and attack you?"

Pearl smiled sweetly. "Then they'll never know what hit them. Don't you worry about me. I can defend myself."

Chloe stirred her cappuccino. "I'd certainly feel better knowing you were staying there."

Pearl leaned forward and whispered, "But let's keep the fact that I'm house-sitting between ourselves." She sat up, "And while you're down in Nairobi, can you get me a kettlebell and a new yoga mat from the sports shop."

Chloe sucked her spoon and said, "I've a growing list of things to buy. It's such a pain having to travel to Nairobi for everything except essential food items and pirate DVDs. I've just remembered, how's your father's duka doing? I haven't had a chance to visit yet."

Pearl sipped her passion juice. "Neither have I, but I presume it's doing very well. He sauntered in yesterday afternoon with a new suit and an enormous self-assured grin. But at least he's doing something. How serious are you about the shop and deli idea?"

Chloe clasped her hands under her chin. "It depends on whether we can find suitable premises, and how difficult and costly the work permit process is. But Dan's away so much, and now I've settled into life here, I'm actually getting bored. I need a new challenge, and something that makes me feel part of the local community. What about you? How would you get your clothes to Kenya?"

Pearl swirled her glass. "The factory in India already supplies a couple of shops on the coast, in Malindi and Watamu."

Chloe looked towards the Jengo Real Estate sign. "Perhaps we should speak to Hellen Newton. There's no harm in her looking for premises for us. But what about money?"

Thabiti had silently been following the conversation, and now Pearl looked across at him. "What do you think? Would you back us?"

Thabiti gulped, "I'd rather back you than join you."

Pearl grinned.

"And you'd need to produce some figures and a business plan to discuss with Dr Emma, before she'll release funds from our trust."

Pearl mused, "I know you don't want to join us, but Marina might. And she's very organised, used to dealing with staff and knows about catering." Pearl leaned closer to Thabiti and asked, "Do you think she'll be interested?"

Thabiti shrugged. "I've no idea. You'll have to ask her."

He turned away as Pearl and Chloe continued to discuss their plans, and looked around the courtyard.

Alex Newton was working on a laptop on the adjacent table, as Hellen and Fergus Peacock emerged from the office complex.

Fergus had not shaved and he ran his hand through his already tousled hair. He said, "I don't care what you get. Just sell it, and quickly."

Hellen raised her arms and implored, "But it'll present much better, obtain a higher price and sell quicker if we clean and decorate it."

Fergus shook his head. "I'm not spending any more money. Just get rid of it." He looked around furtively before rushing out through the entrance gate.

Alex looked up as Hellen approached his table and slumped onto a seat. He asked, "What was all that about? And what's goading Fergus today?"

Hellen rubbed her forehead. "I've no idea, but he wants me to sell the house behind the nightclub before the end of the week. But who's going to buy it in its current state and location. And if they do, it'll hardly be worth my commission. Still, I suppose a sale is a sale and I have to start somewhere."

Two African men with shiny suits approached Hellen and Alex. Alex shrank back, but Hellen smiled brightly and asked, "Can I help you? Are you in the market for a house? Or perhaps a plot of land?"

"No, we're looking for Fergus Peacock. We saw him go into your office," one of the men said in a hard, low voice.

Hellen's smile faltered as she replied, "I'm sorry. He just left."

The other man cracked his knuckles and laughed as he considered Alex. "It's all right, Mr Newton, you don't need to worry about us. The boss is happy with you. You pay your debts, unlike some of your associates. Give his regards to Mr Ramsey."

The two men left and Pearl leaned towards Thabiti and asked, "I wonder who they were. They stick out like an albino zebra in Nanyuki."

Hellen Newton clearly thought the same as she turned to her husband and demanded, "Who were those men? What debts? And just how did you pay them back?"

Alex dipped his chin to his chest. "I thought you'd guessed about the debts."

Hellen crossed her arms. "I know about your gambling, and your failed racehorse, Desert Rose, or whatever it's called. One of the reasons we moved here was to get away from all that. But I don't know anything about those men, or their boss."

Alex kept his head down as he gazed up at Hellen. "Fergus introduced us to their boss."

Hellen snorted.

"And Guy and I borrowed some money from him to pay Desert Rose's training fees, as we were preparing her for a big race."

Hellen leaned back. "A big gamble, more likely."

"Yes," admitted Alex contritely. "But she was hampered leaving the stalls and lost the race."

"So how much money did you owe?"

"A million shillings,"

Hellen looked away as she said, "Oh, Alex." She turned back to him and asked in an exasperated tone, "So where did you get a million shillings to repay him?"

Alex bit his lip and admitted, "From your grandfather's land fund." Hellen was about to interrupt, so Alex continued quickly. "Fergus promised me it would be OK, and there was still enough money to pay the next instalment. All I had to do was pay it back before the final land payment next year."

Hellen exclaimed, "I knew there was enough money in that fund. Fergus had no right lending it to you." Her cheeks turned pink, "And then he had the audacity to blame me and demand more money. I even begged Becky to lend me the money, and when she refused, I got angry."

Hellen bent over the table, hiding her head in her hands and Thabiti watched as her whole body shook. Chloe and Pearl had also turned to see what was happening.

Alex patted his wife's shoulder and looked across at them. He explained, "She'll be OK. It's been a distressing couple of weeks."

Thabiti, Chloe and Pearl turned back to their own table. Chloe leaned forward and whispered, "What was that all about?"

Thabiti scratched his nose and replied, "Money, gambling, and deceit."

CHAPTER FORTY-TWO

R ose turned onto the track leading to Podo School and the Cottage Hospital. Dr Emma had told her the property they were viewing was the first on the right.

She turned through a pair of open grey gates and parked in front of a single-storey building. The plaque by the door had a zebra etched onto it, and Rose remembered the building had been the offices of a wildlife charity or foundation.

A white Probox car pulled up beside Rose and a beaming Dr Emma jumped out exclaiming, "What a perfect location."

Hellen Newton climbed out of the passenger seat. She wore a pair of sunglasses and her face was puffy. She sniffed and said, "As you can see. There's plenty of room for expansion ..." She stopped, turned her head away and muttered, "I'm sorry."

Rose stepped towards her and put an arm around Hellen's shoulder. She asked, "What's wrong?"

Hellen replied, "Some thugs from Nairobi turned up today..."

"Did they want something from you?" prompted Rose.

"Not me, or Alex this time. They were looking for Fergus." Hellen paused before adding, "And perhaps Guy. They were debt collectors."

"But they weren't collecting from you or your husband. So you don't need to worry."

Hellen shrugged off Rose's arm and said, "It's not that. Apparently Alex did owe them money, a lot, and he used my grandfather's land fund to pay them back. Which is why I can't afford the current instalment. I'm so cross with him, and with Fergus for suggesting it."

She removed her sunglasses, revealing her bloodshot eyes. "And can you believe Fergus has been pestering me for the payment for the past few weeks, and telling me my grandfather would lose his land. Yet he knew Alex had 'borrowed' the money."

Hellen walked towards the building and collapsed onto a bench by the front door. "And do you know what's worse? I asked Becky to help me. And when she refused, I invoked an old Kikuyu curse. Don't you see I killed her."

Dr Emma stared at Rose with wide, shocked eyes.

Rose sat down beside Hellen and said, "Why don't you explain why you think a curse killed her?"

Dr Emma handed Hellen a tissue and then walked away towards the boundary of the plot.

Hellen dabbed at her eyes and then looked at Rose. She said, "Becky knew about the history of Roho House. Not the recent battle over title, between her family and the Ramsey's, but the ancient land rights of my Kikuyu ancestors. It was part of the land my great-grandfather was thrown off. She once told me she would help if I ever needed anything.

"So I asked her for funds to pay for my grandfather's land, but she told me I'd have to wait until she'd received the money from her parents' estate. She'd spent all her money on her education, a house in the UK and the upcoming wedding."

Rose sat down beside Hellen and asked, "So what did you do?"

Hellen pulled at the tissue and tore off a thin strip. "I was angry. After all my family had suffered, she was refusing to help, and my grandfather could lose his home again. So I invoked the curse the Kikuyu elders had placed over the sacred land behind Roho House."

Rose leaned back against the wall and said, "I don't believe a curse killed Rebecca."

Hellen turned to her and said in a shrill voice, "But it killed her parents."

Rose rubbed her legs. "No, a plane crash did. The Aberdare Range is notoriously dangerous to fly over. Even if no mechanical fault is found with the Munros' plane, they could have hit an area of low pressure or simply flown into the side of the mountain during poor visibility. I can't accept that a curse has caused all these deaths."

"But if it wasn't the curse, what killed Becky?"

"Now that is a good question, and one I don't have the answer to."

Dr Emma reappeared and raised her eyebrows questioningly.

Rose nodded.

Dr Emma cleared her throat and announced, "This really is a great location, right on the corner of the main highway and the Cottage Hospital road. And there's plenty of land for parking and expansion."

A black Land Cruiser reversed past the gates and then drove in. Chloe, Thabiti and Pearl got out.

Chloe said, "I hope you don't mind. We spotted Rose's Land Rover and I've been intrigued by this empty-looking property for a while."

Hellen wiped her eyes and replaced her sunglasses. She asked, "Would you like to look inside?"

The property was larger than Rose had expected and appeared to have been built as a commercial building, rather than converted from a residential property.

There was a reasonably sized kitchen at one end, male and female toilets in the middle, and a series of regular shaped rooms.

Chloe and Pearl ducked in and out of rooms giggling. Chloe passed Rose and confided, "Isn't this fun?"

Dr Emma, Rose and Hellen re-grouped outside.

Dr Emma said, "It has everything I'm looking for at the moment. What's the catch?"

Hellen shuffled her feet. "The landlord's had a number of tenants interested over the past year, but they've all let him down. So he just wants to sell it."

"What's the asking price?" Dr Emma enquired.

"Four million shillings."

Dr Emma sighed and walked away. She stood back and surveyed the building and its surroundings. "It would be an investment, but that's an awful lot of money to find. And even if I could borrow some of it from the bank, I would need to find other tenants to help pay the interest."

CHAPTER FORTY-THREE

Rose left Dr Emma and Hellen discussing property prices and potential mortgage opportunities. Kipto had helped complete the list of stolen items, which Pearl had started, and she'd promised to hand it in to Constable Wachira at the police station.

Rose didn't know where to find the constable, but she heard voices emanating from the commissioner's office and tapped on his door, which stood ajar.

"Come in," called the commissioner.

Rose stepped inside. Commissioner Akida was sitting behind his desk facing Tessa Newton, who sat on a high-backed chair. Constable Wachira leaned against the far wall. The commissioner had replaced his dying fern with a spiky yucca plant, and Rose wondered how long it would last in the corner of his office.

"Ah, Mama Rose, perfect timing," beamed the commissioner. "Miss Newton was out on the Great Grevy's Rally on Sunday, and Constable Wachira didn't have a chance to interview her. So she's kindly agreed to join us this morning."

Tessa turned to Rose and pursed her lips.

Constable Wachira opened her notebook and began, "One of your group said that you had been rather short with Eloise." She looked up. "Had you fallen out with Mrs Ramsey?"

Tessa sat up straight and replied, "No. Although as we were more acquaintances than friends, it would have been hard for us to fall out."

Rose stepped forward and stood by the side of the commissioner's desk. "I think your animosity towards Eloise was to do with business rather than friendship. Am I right?"

Tessa bent her head and focused on her hands.

Rose continued, "As I understand it, Horizon Safaris was set up by your father, and on his death it passed to your brother. At some point he involved Guy Ramsey who used Eloise's money to invest in the business. But they've managed it badly, bought some expensive equipment, and not marketed it to the right clients. And the business is in trouble again."

"This would never have happened if my father had left the company to me rather than Alex," Tessa spat.

"Your animosity towards Alex and the business may be a mistake," Rose cautioned. "Your brother didn't come to you to invest in the company, did he? Instead, Guy turned once again to Eloise. But this time she was not prepared to let her husband and your brother waste her money, was she? She wanted to be actively involved, perhaps even run Horizon Safaris."

Tessa sat back and looked over the commissioner's head. "I think Eloise would have made an excellent manager. She was organised, well connected and level-headed. But you're right," Tessa looked across at Rose, "I've saved up every penny I can so that I could buy the business.

"I know how useless Alex and Guy have been. But I also know clients who would pay handsomely for the types of mobile safaris they were trying to organise. Yet Alex never even considered me."

"Is that why you made Eloise ill on Saturday? By adding something to her drink after the Grevy's Rally?" asked Rose.

Tessa's eyes bulged and her mouth fell open.

"What was it?" Rose pressed.

Tessa reached down to her rucksack, removed a small container and handed it to Rose. Rose held it up. "Constable Wachira, can I borrow your eyes."

Constable Wachira joined Rose and took the plastic bottle. She read, "Dulcolax drops, a stimulant laxative." She turned the bottle around and read the words on the back. "Can cause diarrhoea, upset stomach and cramps."

Tessa pleaded, "I just wanted to wipe the superior smile off her face. Everything was so easy for her. I've worked so hard to get back my father's company and she was going to walk in and take it away from me."

Rose tapped the edge of the desk. "Why didn't you just try talking to her?"

Tessa drew her lips together and shook her head. "I didn't think she'd listen. And Fergus was winding me up about it. If I had the chance again, I would have discussed it with her, but instead I killed her." Tessa hung her head.

Rose took the plastic container back from Constable Wachira. She opened it and sniffed the contents. "This didn't kill Eloise. And the bottle's nearly full so you can't have given her more than one or two drops. I doubt it even caused the stomach cramps."

Tessa looked up and swallowed. In an uncertain tone she asked, "So what did?"

Rose rubbed her chin and asked, "Did you see anyone in your group with a small glass bottle with a black lid?"

Tessa pushed her hair out of her face. "Someone had that on Saturday. Guy. No Fergus. No Guy.

Oh, it could have been either of them, I'm not sure. Why, what was in it?"

Rose turned to Constable Wachira. "Have we found out?"

The constable shook her head.

The door flung open and Ms Rotich filled the doorway. She peered down at Tessa and exclaimed, "Is this our culprit?"

"No," said the commissioner in a level tone. "Miss Newton was just clarifying a few points for us."

"And what about you?" The coroner rounded on Rose.

"Me. I'm just giving a list of stolen items to Constable Wachira." Rose reached into her pocket and handed a crumpled piece of paper to the young constable.

"I hope you'll all be attending the inquest I'm holding on Thursday morning. I intend to get to the bottom of the deaths of Rebecca Munro, Eloise Ramsey, and their parents, Michael and Geraldine Munro."

"I'm not sure, I have clients arriving," muttered Tessa.

Rose looked directly at Ms Rotich and beamed. "I wouldn't miss it."

She heard the commissioner groan.

CHAPTER FORTY-FOUR

J ust before midday on Wednesday, Rose
entered the single-storey colonial-style
house where the East African Women's
League held their meetings. Today's gathering
had been arranged at the last minute, so they
could hear from a special guest speaker who
was passing through Nanyuki. Rose had been
told that he was a television celebrity.

She apologised as she handed over a pasta
salad, "I'm afraid Kipto's been rather busy this
week clearing up after the break in."

Little Dora purred, "Oh, you poor thing. These
burglaries are so terrible, I can hardly sleep at

night. And I've no idea what the police are doing about them."

Rose leaned forward and confided, "I think they're rather tied up doing our new coroner's bidding. Are you going to the inquest tomorrow?"

"Oh, yes," confirmed Dora, her eyes sparkling.

"So are we," added Birdie and Poppy Chambers as they emerged from the kitchen.

Birdie's hands fell to her side. "Poor Geraldine and Michael, lying undiscovered on the Aberdares all this time."

Poppy rubbed her forehead. "Michael was an excellent pilot. I wonder what happened?"

"Bad weather, I expect," replied Birdie. "That's the usual challenge small planes face flying over the Aberdares."

Dora lowered her voice. "At least we know what happened to them. The poor girls never found out. It's tragic."

The entrance hall was now crowded, and several people murmured their agreement and shook their heads.

Poppy called, "Ladies, our guest speaker's time is limited so please can you make your way straight through into the conservatory. We'll have lunch after the talk."

Rose and Birdie sat together at the far end of a row of plastic chairs. The seating area filled up quickly.

Poppy Chambers walked to the front and clapped her hands. "Ladies, please may I have your attention."

The chattering died down.

"Thank you for coming at short notice, but I knew you wouldn't want to miss the chance of hearing from today's extra special guest speaker, Rob Walters. We're lucky Rob could fit us in, as he's returning home to Australia, to edit a television series he's been filming here, in East Africa. Today Rob will be talking to us on the intriguing subject of 'Survival in the Wild'."

Rose and her fellow audience members clapped enthusiastically as Rob Walters stood up. He wore baggy shorts and a lightweight olive-coloured shirt, with rolled-up sleeves. He turned towards a projector screen and pressed a remote control. A photograph of a smiling Rob beside a crocodile filled the screen.

"Thank you, ladies." Rob's Australian accent made the statement sound like a question. "G'day.

Rob ran through his resume. He had presented a number of television programmes and he'd even written a book. He told them that it could be purchased from all major bookstores.

The next image on the projector was Rob, standing with a group of Maasai warriors. He said, "On this trip, I spent some time in the Maasai Mara. These warriors showed me how to make poison for their arrows from the Acokanthera or poison arrow tree."

He clicked the remote control, and another picture appeared on the screen. "It's an evergreen bush with tough shiny leaves and clusters of small pinky-white flowers. The bark, roots and leaves are all used to prepare the poison."

Rose knew that the Maasai now used their poison arrows as a deterrent to protect themselves and their property. But poachers had replicated the process and their poison was so lethal that a single arrow could hit an elephant, infiltrate its blood system and bring it down within a few kilometres of it being hit.

She thought back to April when just such a fate had befallen a female elephant on Mount Kenya. Rose had helped rescue its infant calf which was now recovering at the elephant orphanage in Nairobi.

Rob Walter's continued, "I've also spent some time with Samburu tribesmen in northern Kenya. Here is a short video of them making poison from the bulbous stem of the desert rose."

Rose sat up and watched the video with interest. A tribesman used a primitive wooden paddle to hack away the white flesh of the swollen stem. He squeezed the pulp, which released a milky substance into a metal bucket. This was then heated over a fire.

Rob continued, "It's important not to breathe in the fumes as they can attack your heart. As you can see, at the end of the process, a thick, black, clay-like substance is left."

Rose continued to watch the video as the tribesman smeared the black goo over an arrow and moulded it into shape with his thumb.

Rob remarked, "Before the tribesman did this, he checked his hand for cuts. Any breaks in his skin would allow the poison to enter his bloodstream and kill him."

CHAPTER FORTY-FIVE

Rose was halfway through her lunch at the Women's League meeting, when she received a call from Dr Emma.

"Habari, Rose. Sorry to disturb you, but Hellen Newton is bringing in a sick cat. She's not sure what's wrong, but it's very agitated. So I might need an extra pair of hands."

"I'm on my way," replied Rose. She wished her friends goodbye and left the meeting.

She pushed open the door into Dr Emma's Pharmacy. Although the plastic table had been cleared, and covered in a clean towel, there was no sign of the patient.

Hellen and Dr Emma were huddled in a corner.

"When I remove this box, you grab him," Dr Emma instructed Hellen. There was a scrabbling noise and a loud hiss but Hellen turned round holding a tabby cat with bristling fur.

"It's all right, Maxwell. The nice doctor wants to make you better." She carried the cat across to the table, but he was reluctant to leave her embrace.

Dr Emma handed Rose a pair of leather gloves and said, "Can you can persuade our patient to come down onto the examination table."

Rose worked her hands around the cat and tried to prise him away from Hellen.

"Ow," cried Hellen as she pulled her bleeding hand away from Maxwell.

Rose grappled with the cat but managed to pin him to the table.

Dr Emma arranged the earpieces of her stethoscope and, reaching down, she placed the chest piece against the cat. "His heart is racing, but that might be because he's agitated. I'll wait a few minutes and try again."

The cat wriggled under Rose's grip and attempted to lean back on its haunches. She loosened her hold as it arched its back and was sick. Submissively, Maxwell lay down and rested his head on a front paw. Hellen affectionately stoked his head.

Rose found a cloth to clean up the mess and noticed green, rubbery leaf like pieces in it. She turned to Hellen and asked, "Has Maxwell been eating plants?"

Hellen smiled indulgently. "He is partial to chomping on the odd leaf, but it's never caused him any harm."

Rose persisted, "But do you have a new plant? One with pretty funnel-like flowers in a shade of pink, white or red."

Hellen looked up sharply. "Poppy Chambers gave me a desert azalea as a housewarming present, and I did notice a couple of leaves had been broken off."

Rose examined the cat's head and neck, and the top of his back. Maxwell shrank away from her probing fingers.

"Look," she parted some of the fur, "Blisters caused by the plant's sap."

"I'd better listen to his heart again," said Dr Emma, her voice full of concern.

She held the chest piece of the stethoscope against the cat, just behind his shoulder and listened. "His heart rate has slowed." She listened again. "It's too slow. Let's take his temperature."

This time Hellen held onto Maxwell as Dr Emma placed a thermometer up his rectum. She removed it and commented, "Thirty-seven point five degrees Celsius, which is lower than it should be."

"What does that mean?" asked Hellen.

Dr Emma removed the stethoscope earpieces and held Hellen's gaze. "It means your cat is reacting to a poison which entered his body when he ate the leaves. Most vets would recommend pumping his stomach, to remove whatever is left in there, but we've no idea how much poison has already entered his bloodstream."

Rose looked down at Maxwell, who stared back defiantly, and said, "Pumping his stomach won't be easy."

Dr Emma also considered Maxwell. "I recently read an article about a human remedy which has produced positive results treating animals for digitoxin poisoning. This is what the desert azalea, or desert rose, contains. It was something made from the glands of a sheep. Let me call the pharmacy at the Cottage Hospital."

While Dr Emma made the call, Rose asked Hellen, "How are you? You look brighter than yesterday."

Hellen smiled, "I am. A huge weight has been lifted from my mind. Tessa visited us last night, and Alex and I had a long chat with her. She's desperate to take over and expand the safari business. She wants to attend travel fairs in South Africa, the UK and Hong Kong, and find new clients.

"It's a great idea, but it's never been Alex's sort of thing. He's happiest organising itineraries and supplies, and prefers someone else to manage the front of house. That was supposed to be Guy's role, but he always got distracted."

Rose asked, "And how is Guy?"

"He's a shadow of his former self. I've hardly seen him, as I leave for work before he's up, and he rarely joins us for supper. I don't think he's eating properly. Eloise's death has hit him hard. Much harder than I would have expected."

Rose attempted to stroke Maxwell but drew her hand away when he hissed. She asked, "Is Tessa going to bail the company out?"

"Yes, and streamline the costs. And what's even better, from my point of view, is that she's promised to make up the shortfall in my grandfather's land payment. I'll pay her back once I start earning some decent commissions. Do you know anyone who would buy the first property I took you and Dr Emma to see? Fergus is desperate to sell it and with a lick of paint, and some repairs, it could be a decent house."

"Just a shame it's behind Stripes nightclub," mused Rose.

"I know. And there continue to be complaints about the noise from that place." Hellen stroked Maxwell and he purred softly.

Dr Emma finished her call and said, "The pharmacy at the Cottage Hospital is putting together a vial of Fab fragments which I can inject into Maxwell. As soon as it's ready, they'll send it over by boda boda. Are you two talking about properties?"

"Yes." Rose turned to Dr Emma. "Did you make a decision on the corner plot?"

"I've a meeting with my bank manager in the morning. And your young friends appear keen to rent some space there?"

"Which young friends?" Rose wrinkled her brow.

"Pearl and Chloe. They want to open a clothes shop and fresh food shop with a cafe."

CHAPTER FORTY-SIX

On Thursday morning Rose parked her Land Rover Defender beside the metre-high concrete wall which surrounded Nanyuki's council offices and law courts. A yellow-coated parking attendant approached her and she exchanged twenty shillings for a paper parking receipt.

She walked past a group of boys who were playing beside the entrance to the council complex. She felt a sting and cried out. The children stopped their game and a boy of about nine, whose toes protruded through the front of his shabby trainers, approached Rose with his head bowed and said, "Pole, mama. I didn't mean to hit you."

Rose wrinkled her nose and asked, "What did you hit me with?"

Reluctantly he held up a small tube, which reminded Rose of the pea-shooter her brother had when they were children. She looked at it more closely and realised it was an empty cylinder from a pen. She asked, "Do you put a stone in there and blow into one end to fire it?"

The young boy nodded.

Emboldened, two older boys stepped forward. "I fire mine using an elastic band," one said, proudly showing Rose his weapon.

"And I have a catapult." The third boy held up a crude catapult created from a fork-shaped piece of wood and what looked like strips of bicycle inner tube.

"Just be careful. There will be lots of people entering the council offices this morning."

"Mama Rose," Thabiti shouted.

Rose turned around and smiled as Thabiti and Pearl joined her. She asked, "Is Chloe joining us?"

"She's in Nairobi," replied Pearl. "But she wants me to tell her all about the inquest."

"Have you worked out how the women died?" Thabiti looked at Rose expectantly.

Rose pursed her lips and tilted her head. "I have an inkling. But I need to speak with Constable Wachira first."

They walked into the council office complex and headed towards a large concrete building. Constable Wachira was standing on the far side of the entrance door, talking to Sam.

Sam turned and greeted them. "Are we ready to hear what our new coroner has to say about these deaths?"

Rose stepped in front of Constable Wachira and asked, "Can I have a word? In private."

The two women walked away from the entrance.

Rose asked, "Do you have the results from the Nairobi lab about the contents of that glass bottle?"

Constable Wachira reached into a small briefcase. "I thought you might want to see this, although it doesn't make any sense to me."

Rose reached for her glasses, which she'd remembered to pack in her tote bag, and read the official-looking laboratory report. A whole list of different compounds were listed, but the one that caught Rose's eye was digitoxin.

She looked up at the clear blue sky and murmured, "I wonder if that's how it was done."

CHAPTER FORTY-SEVEN

S am, Thabiti and Pearl had already entered the large concrete building where the inquest was being held. As Rose stepped inside, and through into a courtroom, she was amazed by the number of people who were already sitting down or standing around in small groups chatting.

Sam stood and waived. He, Thabiti and Pearl were seated on a raised platform under a metal window on the left side of the large room.

Constable Wachira and Rose approached him.

"I'll have to sit at the front with the Commissioner, as I might be called to give evidence," said Constable Wachira. She looked around nervously. "And there are so many people here."

Sam laid a hand on her shoulder. "Just read from your notes and state your information clearly and concisely. And I'm sure you'll be fine."

Constable Wachira made her way, between spectators, to the empty row of seats at the front of the court, on the left-hand side of the central aisle.

Rose squeezed in between Thabiti and Sam. She looked across to the far side of the aisle. Guy Ramsey and Fergus Peacock were seated in the front row.

Thabiti followed her gaze and commented, "That lawyer, Fergus, looks in a better state than the last time I saw him at Dormans."

Fergus wore a grey suit, with a green tie, and appeared composed as he crossed his ankles. He looked around appreciatively, although every-so-often he glanced nervously at the entrance door.

In contrast, Guy was slumped in his seat, staring fixedly at the floor in front of him. Hellen was right, it didn't look as if he was coping well with Eloise's death.

A few rows behind Fergus and Guy were Hellen, Alex and Tessa. Alex and Tessa were whispering animatedly to each other, and Hellen smiled contentedly as she leaned back in her seat.

A voice shouted, "All rise."

The court rose as a resplendent Ms Rotich appeared through a door at the front of the courtroom. Her black robe ballooned over her enormous frame and beneath it Rose caught glimpses of a traditional red and black patterned dress. The coroner beamed triumphantly as she took her seat.

The courtroom door opened and Commissioner Akida strode down the central aisle. He wore his smartest navy blue uniform, with red and yellow braiding around his left shoulder and across his chest, and he carried his peaked hat with its cluster of gold oak leaves.

He nodded towards Ms Rotich as he sat down beside Constable Wachira.

Ms Rotich glared at the commissioner before speaking into a microphone. Her booming voice was amplified as it reverberated around the courtroom. "We are gathered here today ..."

Thabiti whispered, "She sounds as if she's presiding over a wedding."

Pearl giggled beside him.

Ms Rotich continued, "To establish the cause of death of Michael and Geraldine Munro, and their daughters, Rebecca Munro and Eloise Ramsey. On the 28th May 2007, Michael and Geraldine Munro took off from Wilson Airport, Nairobi, and informed the control tower that their destination was Nyeri airstrip. At 11.22 the control tower lost contact with the plane. The couple have been missing ever since."

Ms Rotich paused and sipped water from a glass on her desk. "On Friday 22nd July the remains of a Cessna 172, with the registration number 5Y-VAT, was discovered amongst a forest of bamboo on the western edge of the Aberdare Mountain range. The remains of two bodies were found still strapped into their seats. They have been identified as Michael and Geraldine Munro.

"An initial examination concluded that Geraldine Munro died on impact, from a blunt force head injury, and her husband, Michael, shortly after, from multiple injuries, including those to the head, thorax and pelvis."

Thabiti whispered, "Remind me to think twice next time Jono Urquhart asks me to join him for a ride in his plane."

"I declare Michael and Geraldine Munro officially dead. And recommend the central court rescinds an application, made on the 12th June, to declare them legally dead after they had been missing for nine years."

"Two down, two to go," whispered Thabiti.

Ms Rotich shuffled some papers before stating, "Moving on to the death of Rebecca Munro on the afternoon of Saturday 16th July at the Bushmans Restaurant, Nanyuki. I call upon my first witness, Dr Farrukh, of the Cottage Hospital."

Rose hadn't noticed Dr Farrukh enter the courtroom, but she stood up from her place beside Commissioner Akida and walked confidently across to a lectern and microphone which faced the coroner.

Ms Rotich asked, "Please explain what you found after you had been called to the Bushman's Restaurant."

Dr Farrukh began, "The victim was already dead when I arrived. I had been called after she had collapsed and was convulsing as if suffering a fit. I was told that her pulse rate slowed and she slipped into a coma and died. There is no reason or evidence to contradict this statement. A subsequent autopsy confirmed my initial finding that she died from a heart attack, the cause of which is unknown."

Ms Rotich leaned forward and asked, "Was there any evidence of any injury to the body, which may have contributed to Miss Munro's death?"

"There was a scratch on the victim's leg, mostly likely inflicted when she fell, and a small round cut on her upper right arm."

"And how was the latter injury caused?"

"I'm afraid I have no idea."

"Could it have led to her death?"

"Not on its own. It was no longer bleeding when I examined her."

Ms Rotich sat up and surveyed the courtroom before she asked, "So Doctor, in your opinion, how did Rebecca Munro die?"

"From a heart attack, the cause of which is unknown."

"Thank you, Doctor."

As Dr Farrukh stepped down and returned to her seat, there was a murmur of conversation amongst the spectators.

Ms Rotich grinned as she once again shuffled her papers. "I would like to call upon Commissioner Akida," she boomed.

The commissioner stood and said, "I delegate to Constable Wachira who has been compiling evidence in this case."

Ms Rotich looked about to protest, but the commissioner had already sat down.

Constable Wachira walked to the lectern with her head bent. She smoothed down her navy skirt before lifting her eyes to meet those of Ms Rotich.

"Oh dear," muttered Sam. "Our coroner looks ready to swoop down on Judy. I just hope she holds her nerve."

Ms Rotich demanded, "For the record, please state your name and rank."

Constable Wachira said tentatively, "Constable Judith Wachira."

Ms Rotich glowered at her as she asked, "From the evidence you have gathered, please state what happened leading up to the collapse of Rebecca Munro."

The young constable opened her notebook and cleared her throat. She began, "Miss Munro arrived at the Bushman's Restaurant at twelve fifteen. She was seen arguing with a young man, Otto Wakeman, before she entered the restaurant." The constable's voice became steadier and stronger as she spoke.

Ms Rotich on the other hand looked put out, and she repeatedly touched her cheek. She asked, "Is

Otto Wakeman here?"

Rose watched the fair, curly-haired head of Otto as he stood and replied hesitantly, "Yes, I'm here."

"What were you arguing about with Rebecca Munro?" asked Ms Rotich.

"I was trying to persuade her to leave her fiancé in the UK and return to Kenya."

"And she didn't relish the idea," said Ms Rotich in a snide tone.

Some spectators sniggered.

Otto hung his head.

"Thank you," Ms Rotich said curtly and turned her beady gaze back on Constable Wachira. This time the young constable held it and waited. "Carry on," ordered Ms Rotich.

"Miss Munro was seen speaking with members of her party. A young girl, Mia Newton, took Miss Munro's arms, and they began to dance. Miss Munro let go of Mia, who continued to dance, holding the attention of most of the witnesses. One witness thought that something had been thrown at Miss Munro, but this has not been corroborated. Miss Munro collapsed and was carried to the lawn where she died."

"You said a witness thought something was thrown at the victim. What exactly?"

Constable Wachira planted her legs slightly wider apart and replied, "I only have the information the witnesses provided. The gentleman who made the statement saw something fleetingly, out of the corner of his eye and could not substantiate what it was or who, if anyone, had thrown it."

Ms Rotich tapped her table. "That's not especially satisfactory Constable."

"That is what the witness told me."

The two women held each other's gaze.

Rose found herself standing as she said, "I might be able to clarify what was thrown and possibly, by whom."

Constable Wachira looked relieved and Commissioner Akida turned towards Rose beaming, with an 'I knew you would pull something out of the hat' expression.

CHAPTER FORTY-EIGHT

M iss Rotich glared at Rose and demanded, "You again. Exactly who are you?"

The commissioner stood and announced, "Mama Rose Hardie. She is an independent specialist who assists the police."

"A specialist in what?" Ms Rotich demanded.

"Catching murderers," Thabiti said out loud into the silent courtroom. Those close to him laughed.

Ms Rotich pressed her lips together.

Commissioner Akida said, "Mama Rose has helped apprehend a number of criminals over the past few months. It would be a shame to adjourn these proceedings so that I can formally interview her. Especially when she appears willing to speak to the entire courtroom."

Ms Rotich looked around at the expectant faces. "Oh, very well," she said in a monotone voice.

Rose stepped down from the platform and joined Constable Wachira at an adjacent lectern.

Rose began, "Pens."

Ms Rotich leaned forward and repeated, "Pens. What have they to do with this inquest?"

Constable Wachira turned to her and said, "Let Mama Rose continue. You should soon be able to catch up with her line of thought."

Ms Rotich looked like someone had slapped her with a wet fish from the Tana River.

Rose continued, ignoring her audience as she said to Constable Wachira, "There were a lot of pens around that day. Tessa Newton was tapping one against her clipboard. Hellen Newton used hers to write a cheque, and she placed it on the table when she'd finished. And

Fergus Peacock had one clipped to his breast pocket."

She looked up and Fergus tapped his pocket from which the top of a pen protruded.

"But after Rebecca's death, pens seemed to disappear. Chloe asked for one to write notes, but Tessa Newton no longer had hers. Even you, Constable Wachira, had to go in search of a pen. I think you found one on the table next to where Rebecca had fallen, but you put it back down."

Constable Wachira confirmed, "I did pick one up, but the ink cartridge was missing, and so was the end. All it had was a rubber band wrapped around the empty cylinder, so it was of no use."

"An elastic band. I saw that cylinder after the waiter picked it up and placed it on his tray. And I was shown something similar today by some boys playing a kind of peashooter game outside the council gates."

"Can we get to the point?" an exasperated Ms Rotich asked.

Rose looked up at her. "I think the pen cylinder was a weapon, and it fired an ink cartridge or something similar at Rebecca Munro. It was that which caused the circular wound on her arm."

Constable Wachira tapped her notebook. "But even if it did, who fired it and how did it kill her?"

"For that I think we need to review the death of her sister, Eloise."

Ms Rotich sat up, "I would like to keep these proceedings moving forwards, but I planned to conclude Rebecca Munro's death before considering that of her sister."

"I believe they are linked," Rose stated.

Ms Rotich surveyed the courtroom. "All right, I'll do as you suggest. The first witness I have to call," she consulted her notes, "is a Mrs Hardie."

Rose leaned towards her microphone. "That's me."

"It is?"

Ms Rotich looked at the commissioner who stood and confirmed, "Mama Rose and Hellen Newton were with Eloise Ramsey at Punda Milia Lodge when she died."

Ms Rotich leaned back and looked at the ceiling. "Very well. Please tell the court what happened the evening of Eloise Ramsey's death."

Rose began, "After supper Eloise was complaining of stomach cramps. Hellen Newton enquired about a doctor but was told Amref couldn't fly in the dark. The road to Nanyuki is also treacherous at night. Hellen found a hot water bottle and made Eloise comfortable. However, the pain increased and she became dizzy. I was called, but unfortunately there was nothing I could do. Eloise's pulse weakened, she fell into a coma and died."

Ms Rotich read a report. "A local doctor confirmed her death and states she died from a heart attack, the cause of which is unknown. Mrs Hardie, nobody else seems to think these deaths are linked, so why do you?"

"Desert rose," replied Rose.

"It's a plant. What about it?"

"It is a pretty house plant, which also grows wild in regions such as the arid Samburu National Reserve. And parts of it are used medicinally by those who know how to use it, such as Samburu tribal healers. But there are warriors and hunters who also create a toxic substance from it. The desert rose contains the poison digitalis."

Ms Rotich leaned forward. "Are you saying the sisters were killed by Samburu tribesmen?"

"What I'm saying," said Rose evenly, "is that I believe they were killed by a poison made by Samburu tribesmen, who showed it off to a visiting tour guide, who was interested in their region."

Several heads turned towards Tessa Newton. She spluttered, "It wasn't me. The only contact I have with the Samburu tribe is when they are dancing at a lodge where I am staying with a group."

She tucked her hair behind her ear as she turned to her brother, and said, "But you have a local contact, don't you? He's been showing you potential camp sites and the location of leopards and lions."

Alex shrugged, "Guy met him, not me."

Rose looked across at Guy, who was still slumped in his seat.

Ms Rotich seemed to have regained some enthusiasm for the proceedings. She addressed Guy, "Mr Ramsey. Please confirm to the court whether or not you met a member of the Samburu tribe recently? And if so, did they give you poison extracted from the desert rose plant?"

Fergus nudged Guy, who raised his head and looked around.

Ms Rotich repeated in a frustrated tone, "Mr Ramsey, did you obtain poison from a Samburu tribesman and poison your wife?"

"No," cried Guy. "I didn't kill Eloise."

"But you did get this from your Samburu contact?" Rose reached into her tote bag and withdrew a small glass jar with a black lid. It wasn't identical to the one she had picked up at Punda Milia Lodge, but she hoped it was close enough to fool Guy.

Guy gasped, turned to Fergus, and said, "I gave you that jar. I told you to be careful. Why does she have it?"

"Shush," whispered Fergus. "That's not the same bottle."

Constable Wachira stepped away from the lectern and moved towards Fergus and Guy. "No, it's not. The original bottle, which we found empty at Punda Milia Lodge last Sunday, was sent to Nairobi for analysis and the results were interesting."

Guy blinked rapidly before once again turning to Fergus. "Empty. If it was empty, what did you do with the contents? You said you needed it to take care of a problem you had."

A flush appeared on Fergus's neck and spread up into his cheeks. "I'm sure they're talking about another jar. I still have mine. Somewhere."

Guy sat up and became very still as he stared at Fergus. He asked in an icy calm voice, "Did you murder my wife?"

CHAPTER FORTY-NINE

Fergus Peacock breathed quick, shallow breaths as his eyes darted around the courtroom. The door at the rear opened and two thuggish-looking men turned into the central aisle and stood with their arms folded across their chests.

Fergus saw them and turned back to the front of the court. His face had drained of colour.

Ms Rotich seemed to be enjoying herself. She looked at the new arrivals and down at Fergus, who was clenching and unclenching his hands. She asked politely, "Mr Peacock, did you kill Eloise Ramsey?"

Fergus gulped as he looked towards the door at the front of the courtroom, through which Ms Rotich had entered. Suddenly he sprang up and raced forwards. The two hard-looking men started running down the aisle.

Constable Wachira leapt towards Fergus as he passed her, and she brought him to the ground with a heavy thud.

The thuggish men's progress was brought to an abrupt halt by Sam, who planted himself in the aisle beside the seated Commissioner Akida.

Ms Rotich clapped her hands in delight and the courtroom erupted as spectators began filming and photographing the spectacle. Eventually Ms Rotich brought a gavel down loudly and proclaimed, "Order. Please. Can everyone return to their seats."

Constable Wachira had dragged Fergus Peacock to his feet and was in the process of restraining him with the help of one of the court clerks.

She looked across at Rose, who nodded, and she said, "Fergus Peacock, I'm arresting you for the murder of Eloise Ramsey. You have the right to remain silent. You do not have to make a confession, or any admission, but if you do, it may be used in a court of law."

Fergus looked across at Guy and hissed, "Just because you couldn't go through with it. Would two deaths have been too much for your conscience?"

"Take him away," demanded Ms Rotich.

Commissioner Akida stood up. "Just a minute. Mr Peacock, are you accusing Guy Ramsey of killing Rebecca Munro?"

"I am." Fergus raised his head, and thrust out his chin.

Guy also stood and stared back at Fergus, "Only because you made me. You gave me that pen weapon and told me to fire it at Becky. You told me it was a bit of fun. You didn't say it would kill her."

This time Ms Rotich's attempts to silence the court were in vain.

Commissioner Akida took Guy Ramsey by the arm and followed Constable Wachira and Fergus Peacock out of a side door at the front of the court.

Rose watched them depart.

When she turned back to the courtroom, the two thugs had disappeared, and Pearl and Thabiti were standing beside Sam. Rose joined them.

Sam shook his head. "I hate to admit it, but I rather enjoyed that, even though the murder of two young women is a tragedy."

"I think I need someone to explain exactly what happened so I can tell Chloe," said Pearl, rubbing her chin.

Ms Rotich's voice boomed out of the court speakers.

"Mama Rose Hardie. My office, please."

CHAPTER FIFTY

R ose followed Ms Rotich out of the door at the front of the court, along a corridor and into a generously proportioned room, with a brass plaque on the door which announced 'Coroner'.

Commissioner Akida was waiting inside. "Constable Wachira will be with us shortly, as soon as the custody sergeant has processed the prisoners."

Ms Rotich disappeared behind a screen and re-emerged minus her robe. Rose blinked at the enormous brightly patterned dress she wore. The coroner removed two bottles and some glasses from a cabinet and asked, "Brandy or whisky."

The commissioner's eyes lit up as he saw the single malt Laphroaig whisky bottle. It was a scotch Craig had enjoyed.

"I'd love a small brandy," said Rose.

Ms Rotich poured the drinks and said, "I don't normally like surprises in my court. And I prefer to be told the facts before proceedings begin."

Rose looked at Commissioner Akida before she replied, "I had nothing more than a faint suspicion of the truth this morning. It was meeting the boys outside the council office gates with their homemade weapons, and Constable Wachira's report of the contents of the glass bottle, which sent me on the right path.

"And it was lucky that Fergus Peacock and Guy Ramsey were both in court, sitting next to each other. I'd learned that Guy was devastated by his wife's death. I think he's known all along that Fergus killed her, but he's refused to admit it to himself. Refused to face up to the fact that he could have prevented Eloise's death."

Ms Rotich indicated for the commissioner and Rose to sit down in front of her enormous desk. She handed them their drinks, and asked, "Did Guy Ramsey kill Rebecca Munro? And if so, do you think it was intentional?"

Rose sipped her brandy appreciatively. "I suspect Fergus had been needling away at Guy for some time, and it didn't take much to persuade him to fire the homemade weapon. Whether he thought Rebecca would die or not, I can't be sure."

Commissioner Akida asked, "How did a pen cartridge kill her? And so quickly?"

"I really am guessing," admitted Rose. "But at our meeting of the East African Women's League yesterday, we had a guest speaker who had spent some time with the Samburu tribe. He showed a video of the tribesmen making a thick clay-like substance from the bulbous root of the desert rose, which they smeared over their hunting arrows.

"It hardened onto the arrows but, when fired, infected the victim with the poison. I noted that the outside of the wound on Rebecca's arm was black. Such a substance could have caused that and the poison would have immediately entered her bloodstream."

Ms Rotich sat down in her own chair but leaned forward across her desk. "But why did they do it?"

"Money," replied Rose. "And my guess is it has to do with the Munro parents' estate. Fergus Peacock is a gambler ..."

"Is that what those two unsavoury characters were doing in my courtroom?" Ms Rotich sat up.

"Yes, they've been searching for Fergus, who in turn has been trying to liquidate his assets."

The commissioner said, "We now have the details of Rebecca Munro's English lawyer and we will be going through Fergus Peacock's client accounts very carefully."

"Good," replied the coroner. There was a tap on the door.

"Come in," called Ms Rotich.

Constable Wachira entered the room.

"Congratulations on apprehending the culprit, Constable," said Ms Rotich. She returned her attention to the commissioner and smiled broadly. "Now if you don't mind, I have a press conference to host. And I have plenty of news to give them." She preened.

Constable Wachira walked slowly around the perimeter of the room. She picked up a large gold tankard and lid.

Rose gasped.

The constable turned towards Ms Rotich and commented, "This is an impressive trophy."

"Thank you," said Ms Rotich, who walked around her desk and removed the tankard from the constable's grasp. "Just a little something I was presented with."

"And some nice silver boxes," the constable continued, running her hands along the top of a display shelf.

Ms Rotich moved from one foot to the other. "I really have to go."

The commissioner held his glass up to the light to admire its contents. "The last time I had

Laphroaig was with your husband, Craig," he said turning to Rose.

Rose looked from the tankard, to the silver boxes, to the bottle of whisky and pursed her lips.

The constable faced Ms Rotich and asked, "Where did you get these?"

Ms Rotich's shoulders drooped. "From a shop in Nanyuki. I think it's new, but they sell some wonderful trinkets and household items."

Rose said dryly, "My household items."

CHAPTER FIFTY-ONE

After the inquest, Pearl returned home to Guinea Fowl Cottage. She collected her overnight bag and several folders from her room, and joined Thabiti at the dining table on the veranda.

She said, "So Sam thinks Fergus Peacock was stealing money from the Munro parents' estate. And the English lawyer would have discovered this when Rebecca rewrote her will. So Fergus Peacock persuaded Guy to kill Rebecca, so her money passed to Eloise and not her new husband."

Thabiti continued, "And Fergus killed Eloise so she wouldn't discover how much money was missing. Apparently she was interested in buying out Alex Newtons's safari business, so she might have already started asking about funds to purchase it."

Pearl searched through her files. "And what about the sisters' parents? Did someone sabotage their plane?"

Thabiti replied, "No, I don't think there was anything sinister about their crash. But because they landed in thick bamboo, the plane lay undiscovered for years. When the sisters submitted an application to the court, to have their parents declared legally dead, it probably panicked Fergus and initiated the series of deadly events."

Pearl triumphantly removed a pad of paper from a folder. "Thanks for clarifying it all. Now I can explain what happened to Chloe. Will you tell Marina about it?"

"Yes, and I think I'll do so in person. Despite joking about not flying with Jono Urquhart, he's invited me to join him on a supply run to Kakuma Refugee Camp tomorrow. It means I can visit Marina."

Pearl flicked through the pad. "Will you speak to her about our shop and cafe idea? If she's interested, Chloe can provide her with more details."

Thabiti tapped the table. "If I remember."

Pearl picked up the pad and placed it in her overnight bag. "I'm going over to Chloe's house now. I feel bad that it's been empty all morning whilst I've been in court. As she won't be back until tomorrow afternoon, and you're away on your trip, do you fancy supper at Cape Chestnut tomorrow evening?"

"Sure, and I'm meeting Dr Emma this afternoon to go through our finances and some potential investment opportunities."

Pearl lifted her bag and raised her eyebrows at Thabiti. She said, "That sounds serious, and rather grown-up."

Dr Emma sat at the cedar dining table at Guinea Fowl Cottage and looked out into the garden. It was neat and tidy and she watched three guinea fowl pecking at the grass.

She turned as Thabiti sat down and opened his laptop. He asked, "How was the meeting with your bank manager this morning?"

"It went well, but it's rather scary. I've never borrowed money before and we're talking about a large amount."

Thabiti picked at the label on his Stoney Tangawizi ginger beer bottle. "But you are investing in your business, and a prime piece of real estate. You already pay rent on your current premises, but it's far better to pay interest on land you actually own."

Dr Emma opened her file. "Funny that you mention that. I've received a letter from my current landlord and he wants to raise my rent by fifteen per cent. He says the pharmacy is an exceptional location in the centre of Nanyuki."

Thabiti replied, "He's right. Although the layout wouldn't suit every business. But fifteen per cent sounds steep. I bet he's trying it on. He'll get a shock if you tell him you're leaving. So are you going to buy the corner plot?"

"I think so." Dr Emma removed a piece of paper from her file and handed it to Thabiti. "These are the figures for the land, and an estimate for the work that needs doing to convert one room into an operating theatre."

"I thought you weren't going to do that straight away."

"I won't buy all the fancy equipment, but I do need a sterile environment, with good lighting, for the procedures I already undertake."

Thabiti considered the sheet of figures. "And the difference between your current rent and the monthly interest repayment is twenty thousand shillings."

"Exactly," Dr Emma confirmed. "So if your friends are willing to pay that, I really should take the risk and buy the property."

Thabiti handed the piece of paper back. "I'll let Pearl and Chloe know about the rent, and that you are serious about buying the plot. Land rarely decreases in value. Especially such a prominent location in Nanyuki."

"And I'll have space to expand, and I could build or convert an area from which to sell pet food and other supplies which I don't currently have room to store." Dr Emma's eyes sparkled behind her large yellow glasses.

Thabiti stroked his laptop. "Talking of property investments, I have two I would like to discuss with you. Hellen Newton showed me the house Fergus Peacock owns behind Stripes nightclub. It's large, and wouldn't take much work or money to make it presentable."

Dr Emma pressed her lips into a thin line. "But what about the nightclub?"

"That certainly reduces its rental value, but it also means I can buy it very cheaply and sit on it for a while, or let it out at a low rent. There are plenty of people still living in the area. They haven't all left because of the noise."

Dr Emma frowned. "But they are complaining about it. How much did you think you would offer?"

"A million shillings."

Dr Emma's eyes bulged. "You're joking. That would be a bargain."

"Exactly. Would you authorise our trust to buy the property?"

"Definitely. Did you say you were considering a second investment? You're becoming quite the entrepreneur."

CHAPTER FIFTY-TWO

Pearl parked her green Toyota Rav 4 in an open-fronted garage at the rear of Chloe's house. She unlocked the back door of the house and wandered around. All was quiet.

There was a small bay window in the guest room with a cushioned seat. She removed the pad of paper from her bag, sat down and flicked through the designs she had begun to sketch when her mother died. She'd had such grand ideas of studying abroad and working for one of the famous fashion houses.

She smiled and looked out of the window. Now she was content to create a few simple designs for her own range. And who knew, great things came from simple beginnings. But she wasn't sure she wanted fame or international recognition. She was filled with excitement at the thought of setting up a small venture with her friends.

To start with, she could create a simple, easy-to-wear collection with perhaps a few items for the beach, such as some baggy trousers. Most of the clothes would be for women, but there might be a market for a small selection of men's trousers and shirts. She could expand into children's clothing later, if there was sufficient demand.

She'd seen some lovely scarves, jewellery and gift items when she'd visited India, and opening a shop would give her an excuse to return and chose some to sell. And perhaps Chloe or Marina would join her.

She heard a noise. Had someone shouted and knocked at the door? She listened, but there was only silence.

She picked up a pencil and turned to the first blank page in her pad. She stopped. She'd definitely heard something. The sound of breaking glass and now men's voices.

She sat very still and listened to the muffled sounds. She heard a crash and a curse. She was tense and felt a flush spread through her body. Who were these people? How dare they think they could break into people's houses, her friends' houses, and take whatever they pleased?

She had asked Constable Wachira for her phone number in case something like this happened. She texted, "At Chloe's house. Burglars here. Come quickly. Pearl" She pressed send.

Now for the intruders. She thought she could tackle them with her bare hands, but probably only on a one-on-one basis. There were at least two of them, so she needed a weapon. She'd seen a stand in the hallway which held a couple of umbrellas and a walking stick. A walking stick was ideal. She tiptoed to the door, stopped and listened.

The noises were coming from the far end of the corridor where the dining and living rooms were located. She quickly opened the door, so it wouldn't squeak, and searched for the umbrella stand. Spotting the walking stick, she sprang across the corridor and swiftly removed it. She felt empowered as she stealthily made her way, bare-footed, along the wooden floor of the corridor.

"What about this?" a male voice shouted.

"Ne'er," came the response, and Pearl thought she recognised the man's muffled voice.

She jumped into the open doorway, holding the stick across her middle in case one of her assailants lashed out at her. Instead, they were frozen in position. One black balaclava-ed figure was leaning over a side table. He had been wrapping a figurine in newspaper. The second was squatting down and had been examining the contents of a bookshelf.

The squatting figure reached into the bookshelf, extracted a book and threw it at Pearl's head. She ducked and lunged towards him, pulling his nearest leg from under him with the hooked end of the walking stick. He crashed to the ground.

The second figure picked up a cardboard box and started towards an open door which led into the dining door. Pearl ran, slid and rolled across the floor and jumped up in front of him.

He gripped the box and tried to duck to one side. Pearl matched his movement.

He held the box up in front of him and tilted his head.

"No, you don't," said Pearl calmly.

The figure pushed the box towards Pearl and pretended to drop it. Pearl sprang forward, and the figure dodged around her. She spun and caught him on the knee with her walking stick.

As he started to fall, the box dropped from his outstretched arms. Pearl dived forward, landing on her back but catching the box before it hit the ground. Her assailant lurched through the open doorway.

Pearl saw a movement out of the corner of her eye. The second intruder was on his feet but limping as he made his way across the room. Pearl set the box down, sprang to a squatting position and leapt forwards grabbing the man around the knees. There was a howl and a crash as he fell against a lamp and soon Pearl, the burglar and the lamp crashed to the floor.

Pearl heard footsteps and a pair of large black shoes appeared in front of her. "Would you like some help?" Commissioner Akida asked politely.

Pearl reached up with her arm and he pulled her to her feet. She stumbled as her knee gave way. She straightened it and managed to stand as she worked to control her breathing. Her cheek ached.

Constable Wachira appeared in the open doorway, propelling the first intruder in front of her. She wore a grim look of satisfaction. She declared, "You two have given us a lot of trouble. You've preyed on local residents, particularly the elderly, and stolen their treasured possessions. So let's see who you are."

She pulled the balaclava off the first burglar to reveal a young man with a scar running above his right eye. Pearl didn't recognise him.

"And this one," said the commissioner as he helped Pearl lift the second figure to an upright position. Pearl removed the balaclava and exclaimed "Pa." Without thinking, she slapped him across the face.

"Now, now," said the Commissioner, his voice full of satisfaction.

"No wonder you weren't travelling anywhere to buy stock for your duka," Pearl spat. "You were helping yourself from local residents."

"And selling them to other residents," commented Constable Wachira. "Which, considering the size of Nanyuki, and its close knit community, was not the brightest idea." She turned to Pearl. "I'm happy to report that we've recovered most of Mama Rose's possessions. A large number of them had been purchased by our new coroner."

The commissioner, still holding Pearl's father by the arm, replaced his cap and remarked, "So if she gives me any trouble in the future I only need to mention 'handling stolen goods'. I'm sure the threat will soon wear off, but it might give me a couple of weeks' satisfaction."

Constable Wachira turned to Pearl, "I'll need a statement from you, but first I'll have to process these two."

Commissioner Akida added, "And don't forget, Constable, you have your sergeant's exams in the morning."

Constable Wachira groaned as she propelled her prisoner from the room.

CHAPTER FIFTY-THREE

Jono Urquhart spoke into his microphone. "Prepare for landing."

Thabiti looked out of the cockpit window at rows of shiny, corrugated-metal roofed huts of Kakuma Refugee Camp. The bare-earth terrain was flat and stretched as far as Thabiti could see, broken only occasionally by a scrubby patch of grass, a lone leafless tree or a clump of bushes.

Jono landed expertly on the dirt runway and guided the plane towards a single-storey concrete administrative building.

"I think someone's excited to see us, or at least you," said Jono as he pointed to a figure running out of the building waving her arms. It was Marina. Thabiti felt his heart lurch.

Jono removed his headset. "I'll unload the supplies. You go with Marina and meet me back here at eleven-thirty."

Marina threw her arms around Thabiti and exclaimed, "It's great to see you."

"And you," he stammered. "I have some things for you."

"Fantastic, but don't show them to me just yet. There are too many prying eyes. Bring them with you and I'll give you a quick tour."

Thabiti hoisted his daysack over his shoulder and followed Marina. Outside the airstrip they walked across a sandy area where two tall sticks had been planted in the ground.

"Football goals or a volleyball net. We attach a piece of string across them for the latter," explained Marina.

Two skinny men herded a small group of equally skinny goats in front of the goalposts.

As they walked between rows of dirty-white tents with 'UN' stamped on the side, they were greeted by everyone they saw. Old toothless men and women sat on the ground or on yellow plastic containers and grinned at them, whilst small children, wearing only a torn vest or t-shirt, ran after them and squealed with delight when Marina stopped, spun round and shouted "Boo".

They walked past a pipe protruding from the ground. Several women stood beside white and yellow plastic containers as they waited their turn to fill them with water. A young boy splashed his feet in an adjacent puddle.

They turned into an alley reminiscent of the back streets of Nanyuki. On one side there were permanent wooden buildings with tin roofs. Wooden display areas had been erected in front of them and some were covered with stained tarpaulins, under which clothes, dry foods and household items were displayed.

On the opposite side, the stalls were temporary in nature. Some were wooden tables displaying wares, but others were just piles of plastic tubs and bowls, or stacks of red Coca-Cola crates.

Marina turned right and stopped in front of a corrugated-iron shed, with blue tarpaulins draped across the inner walls. A few customers lounged in green plastic chairs beside crude wooden tables, with gaudy yellow and pink plastic coverings.

"Let me introduce you to Nathaniel. I've helped him start his cafe." Marina smiled proudly.

A round-faced man in his early thirties waved at Thabiti and said, "Hi."

He shook hands with Marina, greeting her with an affable, "Habari, Marina."

Marina and Thabiti sat down, either side of a narrow table. Nathaniel brought Marina a bottle of Sprite and Thabiti a Stoney Tangawizi ginger beer. He removed the caps at the table and said, "Maisha Marefu."

Thabiti nodded and turned to Marina. "There were tents as we walked from the airstrip, but overall I'm amazed at the camp's air of permanence."

Marina drank some Sprite before replying, "Kakuma has a population of 185,000, with people from many varied backgrounds. Take Nathaniel. He and his father escaped from Rwanda when he was twelve, but they were separated and Nathaniel ended up in a refugee camp in Tanzania before moving here."

Two men entered the small cafe and sat at the end of their table. Marina continued, "There is some money in the camp which has its own micro-economy. Nathaniel ran errands and saved enough money to buy a bike. He started a bicycle taxi business, but although he saved up, he was refused credit to open this cafe."

"Are there banks here?"

"I know, you wouldn't think there would be but there are a few, although most money is circulated by mobile phones via M-Pesa. But most of the camp's inhabitants don't have ID, so they can't get credit. A new NGO started offering loans to the refugees, and I helped Nathaniel obtain one."

Thabiti looked up at the small blackboard which displayed the menu.

Marina followed his gaze. "He's starting with simple but popular food. Rice or Ugali, with a choice of beans or vegetables and, if he can get them, beef or chicken. All served with a chapati."

"Sounds perfect to me," said Thabiti, rubbing his tummy.

Marina leaned forward and said, "Now tell me all about the inquest. Chloe said she couldn't make it, but I presume you were there."

Thabiti filled Marina in on the details, although she seemed surprisingly well informed.

"News like the unexplained deaths of two mzungu sisters adds a touch of excitement around here, in the staff and volunteer community. Life can become monotonous at times, although I'm kept very busy."

"It doesn't seem a very appealing place to live. Do these people have a chance to leave?"

Marina shrugged her shoulders. "Some do, but only a few, like those who do particularly well at school or show exceptional athletic prowess. The rest do the best they can. Some families have been here for three generations. They've married, had children and grieved their dead, all out here in the desert."

Thabiti looked closely at Marina and asked, "Are you enjoying it?"

She drew her lips together and nodded slowly, "I am. And I feel I'm doing some good, but it's a drop in the ocean. The problems these people face are far larger than anything I can resolve. But I'm doing my bit."

Thabiti picked at the label on his bottle and asked, "Have Pearl or Chloe mentioned anything to you about a business venture?"

Marina ran her tongue over her bottom lip. "No. What do they have in mind?"

"They're considering opening a clothes shop, with items designed by Pearl, and a specialist food shop with a cafe. And they wondered if you would like join them."

Marina looked around Nathaniel's small cafe. "I enjoyed helping set this up. And part of me wanted to do it for myself." She looked back at Thabiti. "If I said yes, would you help me?"

Thabiti sat back and crossed his arms.

Marina smiled sympathetically. "I know it's not really your thing. Not after Borana. But I'm happy running the front-of-house, and the kitchen, if I have help with deliveries, and repairing equipment or sorting out problems."

Thabiti breathed out. "I don't mind doing that."

Marina grinned. "Wouldn't it be exciting? Running a business together, with Pearl and Chloe. But where would we locate it? Most of the shops in Nanyuki are small and rather dingy. And it would be too expensive to build our own premises."

"I think Dr Emma is buying a plot at the turning to the Cottage Hospital Road, beside the main highway. It has plenty of outside space, for parking and outdoor seating. And the girls say the interior rooms can easily be converted to retail space. There's even a small kitchen. But what about your work here?" Thabiti asked.

"It's not full time. They prefer volunteers to work for four to six weeks, and then have several months' break before they return. So if I did continue here, and run the cafe, I'm sure I could train Chloe and Pearl to manage things in my absence. The key with a cafe is to keep it simple. Like they do here." She looked around. "And not serve chips or fries with everything."

Thabiti's face fell. "But I like chips."

Marina laughed, reached across and squeezed his arm. "Come on, drink up. I want to introduce you to my colleagues before you fly back."

Marina took his hand in hers and led him out of the cafe.

CHAPTER FIFTY-FOUR

On Friday evenings, Cape Chestnut restaurant served tapas, and once a month it hosted a pub quiz. The tradition was that a member of the winning team organised the questions for the following month's quiz.

Rose and Craig had joined a group of friends when the quizzes first started, but that had been several years ago. Rose's throat was dry as she walked into the restaurant premises on a Friday evening on her own.

Sam, Constable Wachira, Chloe, Pearl and Thabiti were standing beside a table on the raised veranda, outside the single-storey wooden restaurant building.

Chloe saw Rose and waved.

"Habari, Mama Rose," greeted Sam. "Why don't you sit at the end of the table."

Rose did as instructed whilst Chloe and Pearl stood beside her laughing.

"So I hooked him with the walking stick and he crashed to the ground. The other one I rugby tackled." Pearl became serious, "But I'm sorry about your lamp."

Chloe waved the apology away. "Don't worry, it needed a new shade. I'm just relieved you saved that box. The thieves had packed some glass photo frames in it, and the regimental statue we were given for our marriage. Dan would have been very upset if that had been damaged."

Rose looked up at Pearl and asked, "Is your cheek sore?"

Pearl turned to her. "War wounds, I'm afraid. That and an aching knee."

"Can I recommend arnica. You rub the cream on the places that hurt and swallow the homeopathic capsules to aid healing."

"Thanks, I might try it. And I heard the police have found the items which were stolen from your house."

Rose smiled slowly, "It's such a relief. I had no idea how much I would miss them. Especially the things that remind me of Craig. The police are still trying to track down a couple of pictures and some books."

Hellen, Alex and Tessa Newton walked past. Hellen called over, "Rose, I have something for you."

She climbed the steps onto the veranda and sat on top of the wooden perimeter wall. She removed a white bound book from her bag and handed it to Rose. "Is this yours? Tessa bought it at the homeware shop before the police raided it. We looked inside and read the inscription, 'To Craig, all my love, Rose.' I know you were burgled, so I wanted to check if it was yours."

"Oh, thank you," replied Rose as she took the book and held it in her hands.

Thabiti leaned over the table and asked, "Have you found Craig's bird book? That's a relief. He was always referring to it, even though he knew most of the birds which visited his garden."

Chloe handed Rose and Hellen glasses of prosecco.

"Lovely, thank you," said Hellen. "What are you celebrating?"

Chloe raised her glass and announced, "To Pearl, for her bravery catching the house-breaking thieves, and Constable, sorry, Judy, for leading the raid on their premises and recovering many of the stolen items." Chloe looked down at Rose, "Including most of those taken from Rose."

Everyone raised their glasses and chorused, "Pearl and Judy."

Judy cleared her throat before revealing, "And we are also celebrating."

"Have you passed your sergeant's exams?" asked Thabiti quickly.

Constable Wachira's ears coloured. "I don't know. I don't expect the results for several weeks. It's not me anyway, this is about Sam.

He's been appointed Operations Director for Ol Pejeta Conservancy."

Sam beamed as Thabiti unexpectedly raised his glass and announced, "To Sam."

Everyone followed his lead and toasted Sam's new job.

"I think we need another bottle," declared Thabiti and headed inside to the bar.

"He's very exuberant this evening," observed Rose.

Pearl turned to her and explained, "He flew up to Kakuma Refugee Camp this morning, with Jono Urquhart, and visited Marina."

As Pearl turned back to Chloe, Hellen Newton whispered, "I also have some good news." She removed from her bag a small, oblong, wooden box, inlaid with ivory. Rose remembered watching Eloise hand it to her in Dormans.

"I saw this on my dressing table this morning, and remembered that Eloise told me to open it if she didn't get the chance to ask for it back. So I did."

Hellen handed the box to Rose and said, "Have a look inside."

Rose opened the box and removed a rolled-up piece of paper. She took her glasses out of her bag and read, "Codicil to the last will and testament of Eloise Emma Ramsey". Rose looked at the date. 18th of July 2016.

She looked up at Hellen. "It was written two days after Rebecca died. And the stamp is that of a local Nanyuki lawyer."

"I know. Read what it says."

Rose read the codicil and gasped. She removed her glasses and said, "She's left you Roho House. Rebecca must have told her about its history."

"That's what I concluded. But," Hellen bit her lip, "do you think Eloise knew her sister had been murdered? And did she suspect she would suffer the same fate? If so, why didn't she come to me for help? Or tell the police about her suspicions?"

Rose considered. "She was a proud woman and maybe she thought her claims would be ignored, or worse, ridiculed. And perhaps her feelings towards Guy went deeper than everyone thought. If she suspected him of killing her sister, she may have been too afraid of losing him to say anything. But at least she can rest knowing that she righted one historical wrong."

Hellen smiled slowly. "My grandfather is delighted. He visited the land this afternoon, but he's actually decided to stay where he is."

Rose asked, "So will you sell it to pay the final instalments for his plot?"

Hellen glanced around before refocusing on Rose. "I think so. Whilst Grandfather was inspecting the land, he met some representatives from Tucan Breweries. He explained the significance of the rear portion of land and they've agreed to protect the burial site, and plant trees around it. And in return we'll sell them the Roho House land. That way we pay for his plot, protect the ancient site and have money left over for ourselves and the safari business."

"Does that mean you'll give up your real estate job?" Rose finished her prosecco.

Hellen sat up. "Not at all. Visiting other people's houses and plots is fascinating. And it's a great way to introduce myself to the local community."

Thabiti placed one bottle of prosecco in the wine cooler and opened a second one.

"Thabiti, are you sure you can afford those?" joked Sam.

Thabiti put the bottle down and removed his phone from his pocket. He tapped some keys and showed it to Sam.

Sam pulled at his chin. "It says Nanyuki Council have issued an order to close Stripes nightclub on the grounds of nuisance and noise pollution. So what?"

Thabiti looked across at Hellen Newton and grinned. "Because this afternoon I signed a contract to buy a property from Fergus Peacock, which is located behind Stripes. And now its value will have at least tripled."

"Good work, bro," praised Pearl. "So now you can't refuse to invest in our retail business."

"So you're going ahead with it?" asked Rose as Thabiti refilled her glass.

Chloe wrapped her arm around Pearl's shoulders and announced, "Yes, Pearl, Marina and I are starting a clothing shop, with a deli and small cafe, at Dr Emma's new veterinary premises."

"Is she buying that corner plot?" asked Rose.

"She is," confirmed Thabiti.

"Oh, that is excellent news. Although I suspect the practice may start to get very busy."

"And that's not all," declared Thabiti, looking across at his sister.

"Oh dear," said Rose. "I don't think I can take any more announcements or excitement."

"I think you'll like this one." Thabiti looked around dramatically.

"Pearl and I are to be your new landlords."

"My what?" spluttered Rose, and she turned towards Hellen.

"It's true. Thabiti, Pearl and Dr Emma signed the paperwork this afternoon."

"And Thabiti promised he won't build any houses on your field whilst your animals are still using it," said Pearl.

Thabiti looked down and played with his hands.

Rose sat back and took another sip of prosecco. She felt it rise to her head. Her possessions had been returned and she didn't have to move. She didn't have to look for somewhere else to live.

Rose thought of the other news she'd received that afternoon. Manager Bundi had personally delivered a cheque for six months' outstanding fees for her work at the Mountain Kenya Resort and Spa. It included overseeing the care of the resort's horses and dogs, and the clinic she'd held on horse welfare.

In addition, she'd received an M-Pesa payment from the polo man, who was building stables near Timau, for two months' worth of orders for her digestive and calming herbal mixes. He also wanted samples of the sports, skin and respiratory mixes. Together they would clear a substantial amount of Craig's outstanding bills.

"So what's next?" asked Chloe.

Sam laughed, "You'll just have to wait and see."

As life in Nanyuki continues, Mama Rose tries to remain part of the community. She attends a local polo tournament caring for injured horses, but when a player is found dead in a stable, there's all to play for if our silver-haired investigator is to discover the deadly truth.

Can Rose unravel the clues before the umpire calls full time?

Click the QR Code to Buy Wild Dog Revenge to score a victory for justice today!

For more information visit VictoriaTait.com

BONUS SCENES

C onstable Wachira looked to her left and right. She stood in a dusty street in Nanyuki behind the main shopping complex and supermarket. At the far end, the buildings stopped and gave way to metal kiosks and a wood merchant's yard. The sound of a buzz saw echoed down the street.

She contemplated the four-storey concrete building in front of her. There were three ground floor shops. In the window of the left one, Tip Toe Butchers, the carcass of a cow hung behind a glass window, and to the right was Shakers Bar.

She looked at her watch. Two minutes had passed since Constables Adin and Ngetich had entered the narrow alley, which ran down the side of the building. She would give them another minute to locate and secure the rear door to the property.

A mzungu lady turned into the street, saw the constable, and retreated back the way she had come. Constable Wachira looked up at Commissioner Akida, who nodded.

As she pushed open the door to the middle shop, she heard a bell jingle in the back room and a middle-aged woman emerged. The smirk was wiped off her face when she saw the constable but she composed herself and said in an insincere tone, "Can I help you, officer?"

"I've heard a lot about your new shop," replied Constable Wachira as she wandered around. There was a basket overflowing with linen and cotton table cloths, many of them embroidered with animals or flowers. Two paintings of zebras hung on the wall. Constable Wachira peered at the artist's name, which she thought she recognised.

She turned back to the shop assistant. "You have some lovely things here, it's just a shame that they're all stolen."

The woman placed a hand across her breastbone as she shuffled backwards. "I think you'll find everything here has been acquired with the full knowledge of its previous owner."

"Full knowledge that it's been taken," replied the constable grimly. She marched towards the woman who stepped backwards into the rear room, turned and ran.

Constable Wachira sighed and waited. A minute later the snarling women was frogmarched back in to the shop by Constable Ngetich who looked around appreciatively and commented, "You've got good taste."

Commissioner Akida entered the shop and announced, "Excellent. Is she the only one here?"

"Yes," confirmed Constable Adan as he appeared from the back room.

"Jolly good. Constable Wachira and I will take her back to the police station to question alongside her associates." He removed a sheet of paper from his breast pocket and handed it to Constable Adan. "Whilst we do, you two sort through the items on display, and whatever's in the back room, and match them with those on this list. We'll deal with the remaining pieces over the weekend. We may need to bring the owners of the burgled properties here to identify their belongings."

Reggie Usman, Pearl and Thabiti's father, and his two associates sat opposite Constable Wachira and Commissioner Akida. Constable Wachira looked down at her notes and read, "Paul Akinyi, and your mother, Fatima." She looked up at the culprits. "So how did you become mixed up with Reggie?"

Fatima crossed her arms and, with a set expression, announced, "I'm not saying anything."

Her son, with a scar running from his right eye, turned his head to her and nodded, "Quite right, it's all his fault. I said we should wait, but he insisted we open the shop." The man closed his eyes and shook his head.

His mother shoved her elbow into his side.

"Ow, what was that for?" he exclaimed rubbing the area above his hip.

"Keep your mouth closed," snapped his mother.

Constable Wachira lent towards the young man and said quietly, "So Reggie's the one to blame, is he?" She looked over at Reggie and back at Paul. "I guess he's the brains behind this operation."

Fatima guffawed.

Paul sat up. "Are you saying I'm thick? That I don't know how to organise a break-in? Let me tell you. Ah," cried the young man as his mother hit him round the head.

"Shut. Up."

Reggie leaned towards the Commissioner and confided. "I knew nothing about the venture. This pair asked me to invest in a homeware shop. I thought it was a good idea, and I'm afraid I never thought to ask where they were getting their stock from. By the time we opened, I'd invested my money, and it was too late to do anything."

"Invested what? You didn't even buy a teacup." Fatima folded her arms and turned away from her two partners in crime.

Reggie lowered his voice and leaned further forward. "Perhaps we could come to some arrangement. You know, I help you and you, well you've caught the main culprits, so I'm sure you can see your way to letting me go."

"Hang on a minute," cried the young man. "You're not walking away and leaving Mum and me to face the punishment. You were the one who provided the list of properties to break into. You've spent a fortune at Dormans eating, drinking and sitting around whilst you listened in to other people's conversations, and found out when they would be away from home."

Reggie looked affronted and said, "I merely passed on the gossip which I heard. You two acted upon it."

Constable Wachira was fed up with their bickering. She asked, "If that's the case, how did your own daughter catch you red-handed breaking into her friend's house?"

"That was most unfortunate," confided Reggie, looking down at the table.

The commissioner stood and paced across the back of the room. He said, "It looks to me as if you are all equally to blame. You two were caught stealing and you," he said looking at Fatima, "were in possession of stolen goods, which you were openly selling."

The three prisoners avoided the commissioner's gaze.

Constable Wachira said, "What I can't understand is why you were stealing from properties in Nanyuki, and selling back to the same residents. Why not steal from elsewhere and sell here, or vice versa?"

Fatima looked up at her, and sighed deeply. She said in a resigned tone, "Because your lot closed my husband's shop in Gilgil last week. I knew we should have waited, but Reggie insisted. Said he needed the money."

Reggie looked up and straightened the collar of his shirt. He held Constable Wachira's gaze as he said, "Talking of money. Please, can you call Pearl and Thabiti and ask them to bail me out?"

"Of course," replied Constable Wachira sweetly. "But I doubt they'll come. Stealing from their friends has really upset them."

Rose climbed the concrete steps to the entrance of the Cottage Hospital.

Winnie Sharpe was waiting inside, sitting on a plastic covered chair in the reception area. She beamed at Rose and said in a conspiratorial tone, "Do you think we could have lunch at Cape Chestnut after we've helped the police? I'm dying for a change from hospital food and I'd love a small glass of sherry."

"I'm sure we can manage something." Rose smiled as she assisted Winnie down the steps and across the gravel to the car park. She asked, "When are they letting you go home?"

Winnie tutted. "They've told me they don't think I can manage on my own. What rubbish. And how do they expect me to afford the fees they charge for staying in the Louise Decker Centre?"

Rose understood Winnie's concerns. When Craig was ill, Dr Farrukh had suggested he stay at the recently opened centre where there was round-the-clock care. She'd been upset when Hellen had told her the landlord was selling her cottage. But she knew a time might come when she would have to leave her home for a hospital room or care facility.

Rose drove out of the hospital car park and suggested to Winnie, "What about asking to put your name on the waiting list for one of the cottages? I know they're highly sought after, but you've been a Nanyuki resident for years. Besides, you and your husband have always been loyal supporters of the Cottage Hospital. If you lived in one of them, you would have your own space but also benefit from the hospital facilities."

Winnie looked out of the car window at the Podo schoolchildren playing football. She sighed. "It feels a lifetime since I was their age."

Rose laughed, "It is."

"I will think about a cottage although, as you said, they're not easy to come by. You have to wait for someone to die."

They parked down the street from the homeware shop. Constable Adan stood outside with a clipboard. He asked, "Do you have a list of items stolen from your property?"

"No," said Winnie in an apprehensive voice. "I was in hospital, so I've no idea what they took."

"And you are?" asked the constable consulting his list.

"Winnie Sharpe,"

"Ah yes, Mrs Sharpe." He ticked her name off on his list.

"And I'm Rose Hardie. Most of my things have already been recovered by Constable Wachira."

He looked at her and grinned. "Of course they have."

Rose and Winnie stepped inside the small shop. There were only a scattering of items on the shelves and a few pictures hanging on the wall. Rose immediately recognised a painting.

Winnie asked, "Have you seen something?"

Rose strode across the room and removed the small picture of an Aberdeen Angus cow in an ornate gilt frame. "Craig had this shipped over from Scotland with a few of his other possessions when he decided to settle in Kenya."

Winnie removed a white linen tablecloth from a basket. She held it towards Rose and said, "My grandmother embroidered these flowers for my wedding. She had to sit under an old lamp so she had enough light to stitch."

Rose tilted her head so she could examine the books which remained on a bookshelf. She pulled one out and turned to Winnie. "Can I borrow your glasses?"

Squinting slightly through Winnie's glasses, she examined the inscription inside the front cover of the book. 'Rose, the best things in life are the people we've known, the places we've seen and the memories we've made along the way. Love Delia.'

Rose hugged the book. With a tightness in her chest and a tear in her eye, she remembered those whose lives were discussed in the book. The friends she would never see again and her dear husband, whose touch she would no longer feel.

CPSIA information can be obtained
at www.ICGtesting.com
Printed in the USA
BVHW031938210123
656727BV00003B/752

9 781915 413277